Lark Farm

- In Flanders Fields -

Other Books by Peter C. Johnson

MicroArray

At The Table

There's A Great Future In Plastics

The Surgeons Are Tied Up In The Operating   Room

H.R. - The Essential Guide To Recruiting and Human Resource Management

I Must Turn On The Light (Author A. Futrell; Illustrations only)

Lark Farm

- In Flanders Fields -

Peter C. Johnson

Illustrations by the Author

Dedication

*To those of the lost who also
vanished in the Great War*

Scintellix Publishing
A Division of *Scintellix, LLC*
Raleigh, NC

Brittany E. Fleming designed the cover.

Acknowledgements

In spring 2011, I spent five days on a cycling tour in west Flanders. Of the sights I saw, most are accurately depicted in the book. Only the names of recognized historical figures from the Great War (Currie, Guynemer, Haig, Plumer, etc.) are real. All other characters, some of the sights and all of the ghosts in the book are fictitious. All references to the University of Prishlatar are fictitious.

Several persons contributed meaningfully to the book. My wife Karen always dropped everything to attentively listen to me read each chapter as it came forth. Pieter Potters and Davy van Bavel assisted me with the selection of fictitious names of persons in Flanders. Dr. David Peters and my daughter, Caroline Johnson, clarified applications of molecular forensics testing - especially the uses of short tandem repeat technology. Drs. Robert Fisher and Pam Kimball provided me with an understanding of rare transplantation antigen clusters. The following read the book in installments during its creation and provided crosschecks on the flow of the story. I am grateful to them for their time and thoughtfulness: Karen Johnson, my mother, Irene Johnson, and my sisters, Mary Johnson, Kelly Jacobius and Monica Sleap. Also; Marjorie Block, Linda Keenan, Hoda Gabriel, Calla Bassett, MD, Pieter Potters, Joan Boyce, Davy Van Bavel, Punkaj Amin, Tomo Aritsuka, Sophie Mohin, Dee Parson Grange, Jill Pergande and Mary Kiczek.

Howard Kelly not only critically read the book but also requested a personal reenactment of Nigel's ride in west Flanders in the summer of 2012, which solidified my capacity to describe the scenes that are rendered. Catherine Hiller edited the initial copy. However, late changes/mistakes are all mine.

Finally, I would like to thank the bicycle shop attendant in Ghent who looked over an entire rack of rental bikes, selected a sturdy red Max Mobiel for me for my Flanders ride, winked knowingly and said:

"This one should do."

Cryptograms

There are four cryptograms sprinkled throughout the text that reinforce the theme of the novel. Enjoy deciphering them.

In Flanders Fields

Lieutenant Colonel John McCrae, MD (1872-1918)
Canadian Army

In Flanders Fields the poppies blow
Between the crosses row on row,
That mark our place; and in the sky
The larks, still bravely singing, fly
Scarce heard amid the guns below.
We are the Dead. Short days ago
We lived, felt dawn, saw sunset glow,
Loved and were loved, and now we lie
In Flanders fields.
Take up our quarrel with the foe:
To you from failing hands we throw
The torch; be yours to hold it high.
If ye break faith with us who die
We shall not sleep, though poppies grow
In Flanders fields.

West Flanders, Belgium

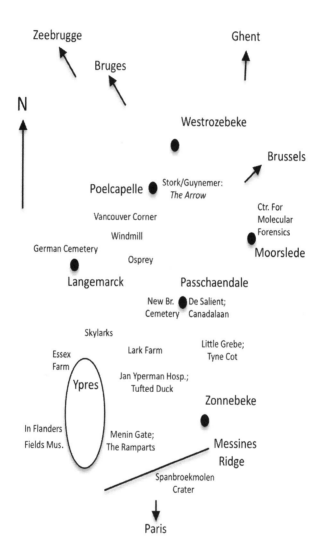

Prologue

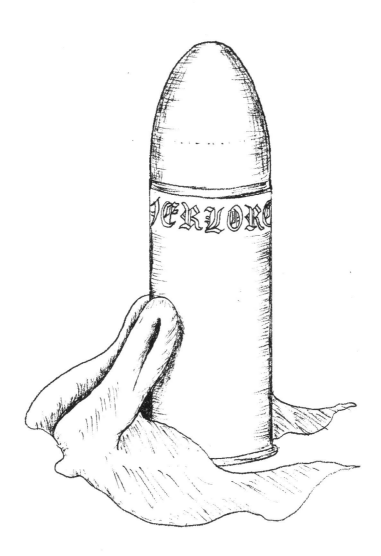

The explosion on the farm near Passchendaele, Belgium could be heard as far away as Bruges, fifty kilometers to the north.

The released energy of the 42cm, 1800 lb. relic WWI German "Big Bertha" shell vaporized Paula Van de Poel. Until that moment, she had been the owner of the combined farmhouse/bed and breakfast inn on whose grounds it had been discovered a day before. Carried with her in death was 1ste Sergeant-Majoor Geert de Smet of the Belgian Bomb Disposal Battalion, who had been standing next to her, moments before. He had come to retrieve the shell for proper disposal at the Belgian Army base in Houthulst, six kilometers to the northwest. Pieces of his truck, its crane assembly and its special sand-filled transport chamber were found as far as 500 meters away. The sound of the explosion rolled like a creeping barrage over the lowlands of Flanders, dissipating finally and softly in France, the Netherlands and the sea. Not a shred of either's body would ever be found.

Farmer Thijs Van de Poel, who had been sowing a nearby field on his Ford 5610 tractor, was blown from his seat and through the closed passenger door by the blast wave. He landed shoulder first in the soft earth and was shielded from injury on impact by the Flemish mode of cultivation, in which deep square furrows are plowed between sow able rows of earth, each nearly a meter apart, to effect proper drainage in this nearly sea-level land. Before coming to a halt, Thijs had leveled six such rows and had filled all of his pockets with loamy earth. His wallet was ultimately located three meters away. The twelve row mechanical planter that had been attached to his tractor had been torn from its hitch and lay forty meters distant. Forage-maize seed coated every nook of the intervening land.

Though mildly concussed, Thijs drew himself up and faced the site of the blast - the front of his property.

It had occurred in the area of the field nearest the road, adjacent to the entrance to the farmhouse/inn. Here, the field was sided by the barn and outbuildings. Marijke, the B&B's Kosovan maid, who had been waving to him from the rear door of the farmhouse just moments before, was now not visible. Nor were Paula or Sergeant-Majoor de Smet, who had been speaking near the site of the shell that Thijs had located during plowing last night. Thankfully, all of the overnight guests had departed earlier. As Thijs ran toward the B&B building, he saw that all of its windows were gone. A four-meter tall fire in the blast area produced a smoke screen that prevented any immediate visual assessment of the state of the barn and outbuildings. As he bounded over row after just-planted row of earth, he began to yell for his wife Paula in shrill Flemish. But he heard nothing in return.

As he ran, he recalled the moment the previous day that the tine of his cultivator had struck the massive shell. It was late in the afternoon, too late for pickup then since the Bomb Disposal Battalion was busy readying the second controlled daily explosion (occurring precisely at 11:00am and 4:30pm daily) of collected ordinance at the Houthulst base. Ironically, the wind was such that that the afternoon's routine, controlled blast was heard moments after he had informed Paula of his find. As they had then together gently whisked enough soil away from the shell to appreciate its size, Thijs noticed Marijke watching them with interest from the second story window of the B&B. And no wonder: It was the largest shell Marijke had ever seen. Later, as Thijs continued plowing elsewhere and Paula returned to the farmhouse to notify 1ste Sergeant-Majoor de Smet, Marijke stood looking at it for some minutes more, then turned away to her duties.

Like all Flemish farmers, Thijs's seasonal tilling uncovered remnants of the First World War's Three Battles of Ypres with great frequency. At least weekly, unexploded shells, portions of guns, boots, bayonets and sometimes bones would come to light in the fields of each farmer in Flanders. This constant regurgitation of wartime artifacts had gone on for nearly one hundred years - and had been experienced by multiple farmers before him - with the same rhythm. And it is understandable, for it is said that a minimum of a metric ton of shells had fallen on every square meter of the Ypres Salient (the famous eastward bulge into the German entrenched defenses in the area near Passchendaele) during the years 1914-1918. Records show that two million shells fell in the vicinity of Thijs's farm alone during that period.

One third of all munitions that fell did not explode.

When Thijs would discover unspent munitions, he always placed them on the concrete slab by the farm's entrance post and Paula would contact the Bomb Disposal Battalion for pickup. First Sergeant-Majoor de Smet was consequently a frequent visitor to the farm. From his tractor in distant fields, Thijs would often see the distinctive Bomb Transport vehicle as it made its way around neighboring farms. Often, de Smet would take a break at the farm to enjoy conversation and coffee with Paula. Periodically, Thijs would join in. He liked de Smet and respected the work that he did. His deeper nature also appreciated the fact that de Smet's sharp wit was a good match for Paula's. His humanity was large enough to know that she needed this interaction to be happy. De Smet to him was, oddly enough, a sort of marital life support system, since he knew that his own avuncular personality could never quite match the effervescence of Paula's.

To provide her guests with a sense of local history, Paula had made a museum of their non-explosive finds in the barn. She was an extraordinary compiler of objects related to painful events. Unusually loquacious and engaging, she enjoyed lecturing about the war to interested guests in an impromptu barn-classroom. She was one of the last Chautauquans. Her guests came from around the world to appreciate the oral history of Flanders Fields – many of them came several times over. All were impressed with her fund of knowledge and enthusiastic style of delivery.

In recent years, she had been asked by some influential guests to attend and lecture at historical meetings devoted to WWI – especially in England and Canada, whose soldiers were the dominant allied representatives in this part of the Great War battlefield. Though raised locally and never previously much of a traveler, she was rapidly warming to this new role in her life and had made some speaking excursions, with great pleasure. Thijs, in contrast, remained the same soil-bound Belgian farmer whom she had met in her twenties. They were clearly growing apart.

As he reached the farmhouse after the explosion, Thijs looked to the right and saw Marijke slowly rising from the haymow behind the B&B into which she had been thrown by the blast. She appeared dazed by the event but declared that she was fine, save for dozens of tiny glass cuts on her face and the back of her neck, all of which were seeping small amounts of blood. Her heavy clothing had otherwise spared her from the flying glass shards, though her hair was riddled with them. She would clearly need a surgeon's attention. She ran with Thijs into the house and she wrapped her neck and face with towels as they then searched the property for Paula and de Smet. But it was to no avail.

Soon, neighbors began to arrive at the blast site, which by then was simply a smoldering hole ten meters wide by four deep. Soil had been thrown in a rough circle radially outward for forty meters, dotting the landscape in a declining but oddly picturesque gradient. Protruding from the deep walls of the hole were twenty or thirty fragments of other shells that had lain there since the Great War. Many others must have co-exploded when the Big Bertha shell detonated. Thijs immediately cautioned everyone to stay upwind of the hole, as often, mustard gas shells were found on the property. There could also be stray, buried chlorine tanks from the systematic gassing of Canadian troops at nearby Poelcapelle, two kilometers away. As some of the neighbors consoled Thijs, others called for medical assistance and notified the Belgian Bomb Disposal Battalion of the event.

An ambulance for Marijke arrived within minutes. Marijke was taken to Jan Yperman Hospital north of Ypres while gloved and masked members of the Bomb Disposal Battalion ascertained that no lethal gas was present. They then began to remove all the other unexploded ordnance from the crater. All of the shells, shell fragments, guns and personnel materiel that are recovered in Flanders have the same rusted texture and a sienna hue. That is why it struck Brigade member Korporaal Koen Van Aalst as odd that a small square white object, apparently untouched by years of burial, could be seen at the base of the crater. He was about to place it in the sand cart with the other material to be detonated but his curiosity captured him and he instinctively gripped it in a plastic bag which he placed into the pocket of his Army shirt. He then returned to his duties, removing the remaining exposed ordnance and readying it for disposal.

As all of this went on, the clouds of Flanders performed against a cerulean blue sky. Large, fluffy and well distributed, they silently flowed eastward in winds unfelt on the ground. It was a normal day in Flanders, except to those nearby.

The year was 2008. The month was May.

The Great War had exerted its tragic reach, once again.

Chapter 1. Nigel

At least, that's the story as I pieced it together afterward.

I am Nigel Hendrick, an Inspector at Scotland Yard in London, where I have worked for the full thirty years of my career. Months ago, soon after my wife left me for our neighbor, I yearned for a respite from work and from my increasingly dark thoughts.

To immerse myself in something new and distracting, I decided to take a short trip and cycle through the WWI battlefields of Belgium, otherwise known as "Flanders Fields."

Maybe I wanted to be lost in time, as so many other citizens of the British Empire had been, there. It is said that nearly 100,000 men from the British Commonwealth forces (including England, Canada, Australia, New Zealand, India and other colonies) had not only lost their lives there but their bodies were never even found. As with most of us alive today, all of my impressions of the place derived from black and white photographs of the Great War. It seemed a vast, muddy void to me. The perfect place to de-identify oneself. And think. I had to see and feel this chasm of humanity myself. Some travel to Florida or to Mallorca. It was Flanders for me.

I left London on the last 'fast' train from King's Cross Station to Hull, barely landing an unreserved berth on the crowded ivory white ferry to Zeebrugge. *Untold Tales of the Ypres Salient* protruded slightly from my cycle saddlebag. It was given to me at the last moment by a member of my department at the Yard, Gilbert Ramsay, a long-standing devotee of Great War history. Gilbert is tall and thin and quiet with a small mouth that opens only when he is enthusiastic about a subject. While I was always a more reluctant observer of such calamities, his influence during our lunchtime conversations over the years had awakened an interest in me. Gilbert spoke the names Passchendaele, Poelcapelle, Ypres, Poeperinge and Kortrij with reverence and I eventually became intrigued by his stories of all-encompassing death, so near to our shores.

While I sat there in the settling early moments of the boat ride, I pored through its pages, so I could appreciate more fully what was to come. A few glasses of whiskey magnified the words, and soon visions of masses of men, artillery and doom filled me. In the end, I slept soundly for an hour on a slat bench near the bar, not so far afield from the duckboard walkways I had just read about.

When I awoke, I was pleased that in the trip ahead I had something of such impressive substance to immerse myself in at this difficult personal time. I stepped out to the rail and looked at the Channel, which was lit only by periodic shipping and the waning sun, behind us, to the west. The ferry rode fitfully on the turmoil of the waves amidst a lowering and chilly sky that May evening. As day turned into night, I returned to and sat in the ship's bar and continued reading the *Untold Tales,* gradually comprehending the enormity of the loss of life in the Belgium theater alone in WWI. The shock did not come from the fact that hundreds of thousands of men died trying to wrest yards of saturated soil from one another: it came from that recurring fact that half of them were never found. There were no remains to return to families. No graves for families to visit, no places of corporeal substance at which to mourn.

Such were the conditions at the front, especially during that vile rainy year of 1917, when the intricate drainage systems of the lowland farms had long been destroyed by artillery bursts. Months of epic rains fell on the battlefield that summer. The quagmire that ensued created an all-absorptive earth that ingested tanks, horses, men and unexploded shells. Only now do these return to the surface, frost heaves and tilling coaxing them relentlessly upward.

The *Untold Tales* graphically described the circumstances at the front in 1917. Movement across No Man's Land required dangerous traverses on duckboards, essentially extended wooden pallets, upon which man and animal would scurry under constant threat of dialed-in mortar fire. The command to attack meant that thousands of men had to queue on these limited avenues that would carry them only so far, before they swam into thigh-deep mud for the final assault, facing machine gun fire. Young men who had never before seen anything more graphic than a Calgary sunset were forced to witness the slaughter of their high school friends while being urged to carry forth - and quickly.

When I finally clasped the book to my side and headed for my berth on the third deck of the ferry, my mind was swimming with concepts of a war that was so wasteful of promising young life. The loss of a generation of the Commonwealth's best had always been pressed upon us in school, but I had never understood its enormity before.

My seaboard bed was hard, and the seas rolled mightily, but I lost myself in a narcosis of pre-sleep imagination involving multiple horrors over which I had no control. Not so different from home, of late. Thankfully, sleep finally came. When I awoke, the ship's bell announced our arrival at the protected port of Zeebrugge, Belgium. Having missed the ship's breakfast, I unlocked my bicycle from its stays on the car deck, donned helmet and poncho and watched as we quietly passed the fateful sandbar where the ferry named *Herald of Free Enterprise* had sunk in 1987, bow doors open and ballast tanks full. One hundred ninety three, my great aunt among them, perished in that cold March water, one hundred yards from shore. It was a colossal example of mismanagement leading to prodigal loss of life. Much like the past that I was about to enter.

When waiting for the large ferry to dock and to open its hydraulic doors, time seemed to crawl. Slowly, the boat crept toward the immovable padded shore, all kinetic energy negotiating with the sea for predictable translation toward ultimate capture by the stays of the linkspan. Craning my neck, I noticed the enormity of the steel doors and their greased pinions, awaiting engagement. Drivers were restive in their autos, hoping to respond promptly to the dock master's throw of the hand. Cyclists were all bundled and helmeted, anxious to launch upon journeys, saddlebags full. The smells of oil and exhaust and the screeches of metal upon metal became full members of the seafaring olfactory and auditory life. Suddenly, we heard and felt a dull thud, and we were in continental Europe.

When the bow door fell, I mounted the bicycle that I now called 'Max' and started unsteadily over the grating that led from ship to shore. As if in Brownian motion, the lot of us, cars, cyclists and pedestrians began our random movement into Belgium, dodging the light rain that fell. Some, like me, started off a bit lost but with maps and smart phones bearing global positioning systems handy, regained our bearings and began a seemingly purposeful march to our different destinations.

The Havendam dock, while initially confusing to traverse, led readily to two roundabouts and from there, to the main artery, the avenue *Baron de Maerlaan*. Despite heavy traffic, I felt a sense of ease as I pedaled along. A clearly delimited bicycle lane accommodated me and my fellow cyclists, a rarity in England. Moreover, the Belgian Fietsroute (cycle route) marking system was sensible: junctions were numbered, rather than were the roads, so one needed only to list a series of numbers to find one's way to a destination. As an amateur cyclist, I came to the continent with trepidation regarding my stamina and direction-finding ability. The latter, at least, seemed to be a resolved issue.

I headed for Bruges.

Chapter 2. Lissewege

The calculus of cycle touring deserves a moment of description.

Upon reaching a certain age, each push of a pedal is a conscious act. When cycling into the wind, even the flats seem 'uphill.' This applies particularly in Flanders, where the lack of obstruction to sea winds allows them to rake the land all the way to the Ardennes. When cycling up hills - and in Flanders, these are generally simply bridges over roads, rails and canals - there is a tendency to try to go too quickly. For the inexperienced, occasional cyclist, this results in acute exhaustion and dismay, particularly when young (and even old) lifelong Belgian cyclists go breezing by. The trick is to keep the process aerobic for you, going slowly enough to allow your legs, heart and mind to agree on the rate of progress. Cycling is a way of knowing oneself, and if that self is not athletic and is slow and untidy in his movements, so be it. At least, these were the conversations that I was having with myself as I rode.

Each turn of the wheel represents progress. Faster than walking, cycling occurs at a speed that seems just right for viewing. No one begrudges a cyclist his view of his or her garden or dress, the way one might if a passing walker showed undue interest. The experience is just quick enough for the observed, and slow enough for the cyclist. Like a strobe photographer, the cyclist clips images from life at a pace that is sufficient to partially digest, quickly enough to never bore. A testament to the gentle inquiry of the cyclist is that at the end of a journey, what is remembered are not the specifics of towns, people, fields and animals but an integrated gestalt of them all. On gray, rainy days in Belgium, that gestalt can sometimes be depressing. But it is life. Just as is the life I was escaping.

Let me provide some background on my voyage. Scotland Yard lies on Whitehall Street in London, not far from St. James Park and the Thames. A month before I landed in Zeebrugge, I took a purposeful lunchtime stroll down Whitehall to the Westminster Bridge and crossed over into the Waterloo section of London, where I knew of a specialty bicycle shop. To the right as I crossed were the buildings of St. Thomas Hospital, where Somerset Maugham received his medical doctorate. Never destined to be a practicing physician, Maugham soon became a man of letters. He wrote the successful play 'Liza of Lambeth' about a prostitute in a nearby borough and once, in his prime, had four plays running side by side in the Theatre district in London. He went on to live an extravagant life on Cap Ferrat in the south of France, treating patients worldwide with his words, in fraternity with physician-authors such as Anton Chekhov and William Carlos Williams. I often marveled at their skills and I thought of Maugham with reverence as I passed the hospital grounds.

Two or three turns beyond the hospital grounds lay Leake Street. Here, the usual slew of local shops surrounded a gem: Haig's Cyclery. As a child in Broadstairs, I had once owned a bicycle and would ride it up and down the Kent coast from Dover to Ramsgate. But that was years ago, on the other side of a long series of bad habits. As I walked toward Haig's, I was stopped short by the sight of a gleaming conveyance in the window: a touring cycle that was so attractive that I was stunned to be able to even harbor such an impression of beauty at my somewhat cynical age of fifty. It was a type called *Max Mobilier* and elegant in a sturdy way. A touring cycle par excellence, it sported the minimum three gears needed for the flatlands of Flanders with a heavy frame that could maintain momentum in the famous Flandern winds. In its aft, it supported a sturdy rack that could hold bulky saddlebags (such as mine would certainly be) with ease. It was love at first sight. It was, of course, bright metallic red.

Having had no recent cycling experience and having been prepared for long discussions with the salesperson before committing my pounds, it surprisingly turned out to be the ultimate impulse buy. In my limited lunch hour, I quickly negotiated a price with the eager salesperson who convinced me to have the bike fitted out with a bell, a light, reflectors, twin saddlebags, a toolkit and a below the seat carrier that held a spare tube, patch kit and carbon dioxide cylinders for emergency inflations. A kryptonite combination lock that could hold a ship in dock encircled the post. I am sure I looked a bit foolish as I pedaled back over Westminster Bridge in my uniform but it was the most fun-foolish I had felt in a long while. As the Thames swept below in its relentless browns and grays, one question remained for me that early afternoon: would I need to lock the bike when I reached the typically well-watched Yard?

I did lock the bike, by the way.

Such were my remembrances of my purchase as I pedaled steadily in light rain toward Bruges. My orange poncho was well designed and kept out all but the most horizontally oriented drizzle. I felt dry, warm and happy as I maneuvered along the bike path parallel to the highway, viewing cows, marshes, and industry, all in equal measure. Periodically, I would cycle past small buildings having low peaked roofs and open entrances that seemed capable of housing only one person standing erect. These, I realized, were shrines. I found them to be ubiquitous - and comforting - in my travels throughout Belgium, a place that seems to need these sites, given its troubled past. Often, they sheltered burning candles, which somehow strengthened my sense that the past and the present were tightly linked here. The Belgians I passed or encountered on my route seemed shy or preoccupied, and none made eye contact. Yet despite this, I still felt welcome, though I knew not why.

I found a cycling rhythm that enabled me to pedal nearly continuously until I reached the beautiful village of Lissewege, halfway to Bruges. Here, in this small town of chalk-colored homes, the Knights Templar in the 1200s supervised the construction of the massive *Onze-Lieve-Vrouwkerke*, the flat-topped cathedral that served as a rallying point for northern pilgrims walking to Santiago de Compostela, in Galicia, Spain, otherwise known as The Way of St. James. Apparently the contributions of the pilgrims themselves enabled the creation of this great edifice, from which precise site they embarked on their journey. By comparison, I immediately felt the smallness of my own pilgrimage.

I parked Max by the entrance to the cathedral and entered the narthex and then the nave. My immediate impression was of a loftier and airier interior than I would have imagined from its heavy external appearance. Constructed of orange brick set off by gray stone columns, the church featured rows of large windows, upper and lower. Beautiful stained glass scenes filled the lower windows while the clear uppers let in abundant light. A high pulpit, constructed of dark wood with a decorative wooden roof, commanded the nave. Beyond and above it, a massive, multi-angular pipe organ seemed fixed in space, surrounded as it was by carved wooden angels.

The only other person in the church was an elderly woman in muted clothing that sat in the second row. Slightly stooped in posture, she had grey hair, trimmed short. Her skin was clearly aged in color and thinness but was nearly wrinkle-free. My assumption that she was praying was belied when I walked past: she was painting small watercolor renditions of scenes from the stained glass. She looked up, appeared to regard me carefully, smiled and without saying a word gave me one. Astonished at her generosity, I thanked her in both

English and in my very recently assimilated rudimentary Dutch. As I left the church, I purchased a small book describing its interior. In reading it, I learned that the image she had painted was of the House of David, surrounded by twelve icons representing the Lost Tribes of Israel.

I tucked the watercolor into my saddlebag within the pages of *The Untold Tales*, and then Max and I wheeled lazily through the town for a bit. In the small Visitors *(Bezoekers)* Center I found a brochure describing the local history. Lissewege was founded in AD 900 after the creation of local dikes. Like many towns and cities in Flanders, it became a major cloth-making center before its economy was destroyed in the Religious Wars. Now it is an artists' colony. I had the occasion to meet one of its artists when I wheeled Max to the front of a covered café, called *De Dame,* which faced the cathedral. She was a pretty Belgian woman in her twenties, originally from Lille, Belgium, who had come to Lissewege to develop her unique style of oil pastel art. We spoke briefly, and then I retrieved and showed her the watercolor I had been given. She smiled and told me that the mystery painter was Mary Van Hoop. Mary was well known throughout Flanders for her paintings of stained glass scenes, which she would always give to strangers. This had been her practice one day each week since she had lost her father and both brothers in World War II in some distant entrenchments whose locations the Germans never divulged. Nelly was her name.

Touting its own microbrewery, *De Dame* was one of those delightful tightly composed cafes that was visibly proud of itself. *De Dame* in midmorning supports a polyglot of tastes. At one table are the tea drinkers, at another, the coffee drinkers, and at yet another the Duvel and Jupiler drinkers - they being the famous 10+% alcohol-content Belgian beers. Finally, there are the *De Dame* microbrew drinkers - those who have the fortitude to face 13% alcohol at this hour of the day. I opted for the tea corner (for warmth) and Nelly joined me. The waiter delivered to each of us the tea with an unexpected but welcome chocolate cracker perched on the saucer by its side. Nelly sat with a Belgian elegance, upright with her scarf carefully coiled and threaded about her neck. She drank her tea with two fingers as though taught this style for generations. I asked to see her artwork and she shared with me her sketchbook. One image, oddly, depicted the town in the absence of the church. As I comprehended the scene, I looked up and smiled. "I must be going," she said, as she retrieved her things and headed toward a group of friends with a light foot.

I must admit that I spent my short stay in the cafe thereafter delivering many a longing glance toward the beer drinkers. I soon dispatched the cracker, checked my watch and departed, wondering about the radial geographic penetrance into nearby towns of these local beers.

I was getting thirsty.

Chapter 3. Bruges

As I pedaled past the sign indicating that I had reached the outskirts of Lissewege, I began to notice poppies blooming here and there. Made famous by Dr. John McCrae's battlefield poem "In Flanders Fields," they bore the red of well-oxygenated blood. How appropriate this color has come to be, relative to their historical role. Poppies, a wildflower in Flanders, could be seen growing in odd nooks, on embankments, near culverts and in any area of untended disturbed ground, flopping fitfully in the wind. It was their ability to flourish in broken ground that made them the flower of the Great War in Flanders.

Today, they are rare to see in the well-plowed and well-sown fields of Flemish farms. I would later see them between the headstones of Commonwealth graves as I drew closer to the historic front lines, but nowhere are they seen today with the prevalence that once prompted McCrae to write:

> "In Flanders Fields the poppies blow
> Between the crosses row on row"

after he had witnessed the death of his good friend Lt. Alexis Helmer in a fatally accurate shelling. Helmer, dismembered in the blast, was brought back together for burial in a heap by McCrae himself. McCrae wrote the poem amidst the poppies at Essex Farm near Boezinge during the Second Battle of Ypres, in May 1915. McCrae, an academic pathologist who had taught at Dartmouth and McGill Universities, was, ironically, serving as both a field surgeon and artillerist for the Canadian forces. He did not survive the war, having died of pneumonia in northern France in 1918. He is buried in Wimereux Cemetery, near Boulogne-sur-Mer, France, essentially as close to Canada as the continent would allow.

Only rescued from obscurity by a fellow officer after McCrae had torn it from his notebook, the poem was anonymously published in *Punch* in December 1915. McCrae was only identified as its author in Punch's annual index. By then, *In Flanders Fields* had become a defining poem of the war. In some way, my regard for the poem and all that it signifies prompted my own travel to Flanders as I first heard the poem as a very young boy, when I held my Grandfather's mementoes of the war in my hands - a discharged 88 shell, a musette bag, his infantry jacket and a well-preserved Kaiser's helmet.

After another hour of steady cycling, the rain had stopped; the sun was out and steam rose from the bike path. I stowed my poncho in a handy pocket in my right saddlebag and I absorbed the beautiful breeze as I swept along. Soon, I approached the southwest medieval gate of Bruges after crossing the city's encircling canal. Immediately, I was surrounded by street after street of buildings that had survived for centuries, unscathed by either war or their inhabitants. Stepped, peaked front walls were the norm, with many of the buildings displaying ornate metalwork in the forms of scrolls, birds and flora. When I glided into the Marktplatz, I looked up at the imposing city tower of Bruges – the Belfry, noting its particular octagonal capping spire and its very slight eastward lean.

Clotted tourist groups meandered about, taking in the sun and the splendid historical sights. As it was noontime, many drifted toward the cafes that line the bases of the buildings on the square. I locked Max and took a seat at the front of the *Cafe Elisien* and enjoyed a full view of the square as I sipped a glass of Montreux. The Belfry seemed to continuously inhale the hearty and discharge the weary from its bosom. No wonder, I thought, as I read the local guide. Built initially in 1240, it contained 366 steps. The Belfry, burnt and rebuilt multiple times over the years, contrasted sharply with the fate of Bruges as a whole during that time, which as a result remains well preserved and therefore attractive to tourists worldwide.

Mostly what I thought about as I sat there alone and unnoticed was how lucky Bruges was to have particularly escaped the horrors of the two World Wars. Where barrages had decimated the buildings and population of Ypres, Antwerp, Liege and Namur, the geography of war had spared Bruges twice. How close does chance live? For Bruges, perhaps a mere thirty kilometers, for there the front line lay. Soon, I would be immersed in that alternate geography, the grounds of the Great War, with all its fascinating and perilous history.

To that end, I made a call to Chief Inspector Wouter Deert, head of the Politie in Passchendaele, about fifty kilometers to the southwest. Wouter had spent some time at the Yard in his younger years, accruing investigative skills to bring back to Belgium. He focused on molecular forensics, then an early art. We worked closely together and had enjoyed many a night out in London with our wives before he moved back to Flanders in the late nineties. We had kept up with one another through the years, and I had recruited his assistance after the 2005

London Subway bombings.   Since then his lovely wife Anna had succumbed to cancer and mine to another lover. So it was as aging bachelors that we spoke a month ago when I informed him that I would be in the area.

He had immediately recommended that I stay at Lark Farm as a guest in their attached Bed and Breakfast. Lark Farm is a working farm lying in the middle of what was once No Man's Land, now an exceptionally fertile farming area. He described the owners, Paula and Thijs as wonderful, welcoming Belgians but he also pointed out that they were intensely opposite in temperament: he, a prototypically quiet, unassuming Belgian farmer and she, the pinnacle of extroversion and volubility. I verified this later that day when she and I spoke on the telephone to secure the reservation. She spoke non-stop, in perfect, enthusiastic English, about the area's unique history and the quality of the sights and cycling. I find it rare to have a person emboss his or her personality upon me so rapidly and deeply, so I was intrigued to have the opportunity to meet this unusual woman in person.

Wouter answered his cell phone promptly, as usual, with a clipped "Goeden Dag" followed by his title. "It's me, Nigel," I said. "I've made it across the Channel and am looking forward to seeing you when I arrive in Passchendaele on my shiny new Max Mobilier cycle! Will you have time for dinner together?" Wouter replied with his characteristic warm bellow: "Of course, Nigel - and I know just the place. There is a new restaurant in Poelcapelle whose chef is creating some dishes that will astonish you - and of course the Duvel and wines will be fine, too." I smiled and indicated that I liked the plan. He continued: "You are staying at Lark Farm, correct?" I concurred. He then said: "Depending upon when you get in, plan for at least forty-five minutes with Paula, as she holds court with all the guests every afternoon for at least that long, over tea and her 'patented' pear cake." Then he said - "But before dinner, let's meet for a drink at *De Salient*, my favorite pub in Passchendaele, to give you a preliminary feeling of the town." I agreed to meet him there in the early evening. After all, at this time of the year, the Flanders sky remains light until 10 pm.

I finished my drink and paid the waiter with a slight tip (I was surrounded by American tourists, after all, and needed to keep up with this unnecessary behavior of theirs).   I then clattered over the cobblestones of the square toward the canal path, where I turned south. Within minutes, I passed the 13th century *Beguinage* at the southernmost tip of the city, relic of that odd culture in which lay women could live communally like nuns, yet come and go as they desired. I then broke free into the byways of Flanders for the last leg of my journey, down a long, featureless motorway.

Chapter 4. Langemarck
And Poelcapelle

On and on I rode in both sun and rain, as the Flemish wind beat against me, coming directly into my face from the southwest. Humbly garbed Belgian grandmother after grandmother passed me with ease but also without condescension. As I pedaled south through Torhout, I noticed a stately building in the midst of the square that houses, among other things, a temporary employment agency. Max and I then traversed slightly hilly country to the town of Kortemark, with its well-situated *Den Abend* restaurant. I stopped there and took hot chocolate on the patio in the sun while visually dissecting the small cathedral across the street. I then pressed on to Langemarck, in whose outskirts I stopped and parked Max by a low arch composed of interesting, massive brown blocks that formed a gateway arch. I stepped through them into an oasis of shade and black stones.

It was the German military cemetery of Langemarck.

Barely 100 meters long by 50 meters deep, it held the remains of greater than 40,000 German dead, the vast majority huddled within a central mass grave - the *Kameraden Grab*, or Comrades' Grave. This central, common grave is made prominent by Scharfes S-scripted black stones surrounding its center that are riddled with Saxon names of the unknowns lost in the quagmires that defined the war nearby. Of the known, it appeared that so few were identified that their stones lay flat and largely distant from one another on the remaining earth of the enclosed site. In fact, each stone lies atop the grave of eight soldiers, including the 3000 student volunteers who had marched, arm in arm to the front, singing martial songs, early in the war. They were mowed down mercilessly by the professional British troops that they were unfortunate enough to meet in those early, hectic days of battle before the armies dug their trenches.

The cemetery is often called Der *Studentenfriedhof* (Student Cemetery) in their honor. Both sides learned early in the war that separating 'pals' from the same schools or locales was a good idea, after the 'Pals Battalions' were decimated, leaving whole villages and towns without men after the war for decades. The immensity of local loss at home in the opposing countries was too overwhelming to bear when whole regiments were extinguished concurrently by artillery, machine guns and disease.

Their headstones, dark and horizontal by decree of the victors, lay silent beneath the plane trees and their forgiving shade. In the rear of the cemetery, minimalist figures of four men in sculpture arose, silhouetted against the backdrop of the fields in which German men fought and died. They stood priestly - erect, dignified and anonymous. It was Emil Krieger's powerful work, the famous *Mourning Soldiers*. Created from a photograph taken at a graveside service during the war, one of the four soldiers it depicts was lost in a battle merely two days later. When viewed face on, he is the second from the right.

The Langemarck German cemetery was just the first of many cemeteries I would visit in the region within days, including the New British Cemetery near Passchendaele, the Poelcapelle British Cemetery and of course, the famous and massive Tyne Cot Cemetery near Passchendaele, whose rear walls display the names of the 36,000+ Commonwealth soldiers who were never found during the period between mid 1917 and the end of the war in November 1918. The names of the other 56,000 Commonwealth men lost and never found between 1914 and 1917 are engraved on the walls of the famous Menin Gate in Ypres, ten kilometers south.

Like me, you may wonder how so many men can simply be lost in a war that is being fought across a relatively narrow expanse of mostly flat land. The answer is simple.

The earth swallowed them.

It swallowed them whether they were intact or in pieces. Such were the conditions of the front in Belgium during the war: a soft, moist, all embracing, sucking earth that absorbed shells, horses and men alike with impunity. Most remain where they lay, though some are on the move.

Upward.

As I entered the town of Poelcapelle, I marveled at the monument standing proudly in its tiny square - a large black stork on a tower, lifting off. It was as black as coal and was too large for even its imposing plinth. Its discrete features were difficult to determine, as if it were asking that the birth of the future be successful and that the horrors of the past not be so closely scrutinized. It was, in fact, a monument to the famous, charismatic French ace Georges Guynemer, who was shot down nearby on September 11, 1917 after three years of aerial warfare - including 600+ sorties in all. He was the leader of the Spa 3, a unit of the famous Flying Storks (known as the *Cygognes*). In a fitting gesture, the reverent Belgian airmen who erected the monument in his honor pointed the stork in Guynemer's last known flight direction. He and his aircraft, the *Vieux Charles* were never found.

A British barrage obliterated the area shortly after his crash.

He and his aircraft, similar to so many others, were simply absorbed by Flanders.

I was in the true battlefield of the Great War, where every inch of ground was sacrificial. I stopped for a drink on Poelcapellestraat, just meters from a turn that was dominated by the town's bakery. Looking to the east, I saw a shallow depression of farmland backed by the so called Passchendaele 'ridge,' a gentle elevation of perhaps thirty meters, upon which sat the picturesque town of Passchendaele and its centrally located, blockish church spire. A close look toward the south of the town provided a glimpse of the low lying, coffin-like Canadian memorial, marking the site on the ridge upon which exhausted, mud-slaked Canadian warriors finally fell onto the incumbent Germans and prevailed, in October/November, 1917, marking the end of the Third Battle of Ypres. Their victory was dear - costing them tens of thousands of colleagues lost in the rotting stew of earth, below. Notably, none other than Adolf Hitler fought in the Battle of Passchendaele, thus linking the great losses here to the greater losses of the future.

Experiencing this part of Flanders for the first time, a great sense of irony and tragedy overtook me. I realized that but for the passage of years, I would be in the thick of a slaughter that man had never previously experienced. Never before had the contrivances of battle ensured that men would be physically lost on an epic scale, their bodies never to be found again. Under the cloud of these thoughts, I pedaled along ill-used lanes to Lark Farm, then visible in the subtle hollow between Poelcapelle and Passchendaele.

No Man's Land.

Chapter 5. Lark Farm

Today, Lark Farm lies in the middle of one of the richest farmlands on earth, perhaps the only land on earth so well fertilized by human beings. When one is normally sedentary, at the end of a long day of riding, accomplishment and the desire for drink fuse within one. This was my state as I rode into the broad driveway and parking lot of the farmhouse and inn. As I slowed by the entrance to the driveway, I noticed the flat concrete panel by the road bearing rusty scallops of metal, as well as the unplowed portion of land to my right. I asked myself why these features had captured my attention. "Because you an investigator, you idiot," my irreverent subconscious answered.

I had reached Lark Farm.

Standing bestride Max, feet on the ground, I spent several minutes surveying the inn, barn, family home and environs. It was immediately apparent that this was a working farm. The buildings were arrayed to foster the movement of large farm machinery, which lay all about. Like most Flanders farms, the buildings were low-lying to avoid the wind and were constructed of red brick and roofed with red tiles. The major farm buildings had large, open and welcoming doors, though no beings came and went except supercilious cats and energetic flies. The farmhouse, in contrast, looked as all farmhouses do, all shut tight as a sealed envelope.

The grounds between the farmhouse, barn and outbuildings were of highly compacted dirt and gravel. Max Mobilier had twisted a bit as he hit the odd large stone while entering the courtyard. In the distance, a man on a tractor was plowing the field. Despite the distance, the wind carried the sounds of his work to me. I stopped and watched for a while as his plow scythed the earth, lifting small tufts of dust that gushed gently away. Why I felt this I do not know, but he seemed to be content. I wondered if he thought much about the land he cultivated, about what had been spent to enrich it, those years ago.

Sated by my initial observations, I unseated myself from Max, dropped the kickstand, unleashed my saddlebags and strode toward the bed and breakfast building, with its colorful flags and signage.

When I knocked at the door, I was greeted by a tall, angular redheaded woman whose cry "We have all been waiting for you" swept me along into a room with a great table surrounded by eight other guests, all drinking tea or coffee and eating cakes.

She was Paula, of course.

I was rapt as she introduced me to a welcoming international group: a pair of Belgians, four middle aged British men and a Canadian couple from Calgary. I sat between the latter and the Brits while Paula quickly filled my place setting with a pot of tea and a slice of her reportedly famous pear cake. She then took her place at the head of the table and served for the next half an hour as a font of local knowledge and enthusiasm.

The Brits paid the most ardent attention to Paula, as they were WWI history zealots who had been to the farm multiple times before. Paula went on and on about the divisions and regiments of each army that fought here, the fate of the farm, the date and manner of its retaking from the enemy and the subsequent years of recovery in the region. The Belgian couple, who were in the area only to look for retirement housing, remained largely silent. They were from Namur in the Wallonian, French-speaking section of Belgium and spoke Flemish and English only sparingly. The Canadians, Helen and James MacCormick, were in Flanders on a pilgrimage to see where James's grandfather had fought in the Third Battle of Ypres near Passchendaele and where James had also lost two great uncles, one having been buried in the New British Cemetery near Passchendaele. The other, who was lost in the war, has his name inscribed on the Menin Gate in Ypres. Like so many descendants of soldiers in the Great War, Helen and James had plans to lay a wreath of poppies during the formal remembrance ceremony at the Menin Gate, the next night.

Meanwhile, Paula was fascinating. And she knew she was.

She described her upbringing on a farm close to Langemarck. She and her husband Thijs had by custom married young and then settled as tenants on Lark Farm. They had several children, all of whom were doing very well and living in the region except for their eldest son, Pieter, a Belgian Military Korporaal who was lost on assignment in the turbulent years of the NATO occupation of Kosovo after the 1999 conflict there. His remains were never found. I noticed that Paula's unique tempo stalled a bit as she mentioned him.

She swiftly moved on to other topics in the conversation.

Prior to WWI, a Belgian noble family had owned Lark Farm. They had fled in the face of the rapid German advance in the autumn of 1914. The German Army had occupied the farm as a command post in the early months of the subsequent fighting but the Germans soon thereafter retreated to the relative safety of the Passchendaele Ridge, one kilometer to the east. Hence, the farm became the epicenter of No Man's Land.

Lowering her voice, Paula described the circumstances at that time: "The shells would fall, day and night. Whenever there was movement on the land, carefully aimed guns would fire, guaranteeing that daylight patrols were vanquished immediately. She then asked everyone to stand by the south-facing windows of the dining room as she pulled back the Bruges lace curtains. In the distance, one could see low rises in the land. "There," she said, "Lie the 'mountains' of Flanders. The Germans occupied the Messenes Ridge until one day in 1917, when the simultaneous explosion of mines that had been laid months before by Sappers blew up the entire ridge. The Australian and New Zealand forces who rushed the ridge then took many German prisoners." As she said this, she threw her arms in the air, as if to emulate the explosion, her fingers wiggling like airborne soldiers and masses of earth.

"The combined explosion was so loud that it was heard as far away as London," she continued. "Just slightly to the east lies deadly Hill 60. It is actually an artificial hill, built from castoff earth when the rail line was built between Ypres and Comines. In those days, the steam engines did not have the power to crawl up even the mild slope of the Messines Ridge, so the track elevation had to be reduced and the earth had to be relocated. The Germans occupied Hill 60 early in the war and thereafter it became a site of to- and fro-fighting in which many men were lost and simply never found. The soft, immaturely laid earth swallowed them as rapidly as artillery could dig their graves. You should visit Hill 60, since it is one of the few sites in Flanders whose terrain still bears all the scars of bombardment, making the process of death more visible there."

Paula then walked us to the east facing windows of the room and pointed to the church spire in Passchendaele. "You can barely make out the rise in the land that made Passchendaele such a strategic location for the Germans, but it was sufficient to hold the Allies at bay for four years," she said. "You must visit the church and see the north-facing stained glass window. It is the most beautiful in all of Flanders. On your way, imagine being one of the Canadian soldiers who fought their way to that hill in the autumn of 1917, struggling through waist-deep mud and fighting against dug-in machine guns and zeroed-in mortars and assorted other artillery. Thousands of men were lost conquering a mere 900 meters, some of whom lie on our farm."

She then went on: "It is customary in Belgium for us to try to do much and say little. It may be that we have been overrun so often in history that we have learned to keep our heads down. Or it may be a little bit of humility - having seen so many men from all parts of the world lay down their lives for us. Having grown up nearby, I never felt that my voice would ever be heard outside of my own small circle of family and friends. I was content for this to be so. But when we opened our B&B, persons from all over the world came to witness this place - where so many men came from afar and were lost. I realized that this phenomenon had touched me from my youth, and I became committed to conveying it to others, particularly once we lost our son in a similar way. Think of it: mothers from all over the world learned that their sons had died but that they had no remains through which to achieve closure, no grave at which they could pay their respects. It is said that an untold number of parents worldwide went quietly mad as a result. I suppose that Thijs and I retain our sanity simply by sharing this experience with you." She looked deeply at each of us.

It was a remarkable personal experience.

Just then I noticed a hard but attractive fortyish-looking woman in the hallway who motioned to Paula for her attention. Paula briefly conferred with her and then, as a second thought, brought her into the room with the rest of us and introduced her. "Everyone," she said, "This is Marijke, our maid. She joined us from the Balkans three years ago and has made my life very much easier since then."

I looked up and considered her. She was a small and thin, a bird-like woman, whose eyes darted quickly about, oddly in the absence of any evident danger or stimulus. Her hair was dark and was cut very short, perhaps even shorter than was attractive for her figure. She wore a navy blue skirt and a white blouse that covered small breasts. Despite her size, she conveyed a certain strength. She did not fidget so much as to move languidly and randomly, as though she was used to using her hands in purposeful ways but did not need them so occupied at this moment.

I looked carefully at her hands.

Her fingers were long and thin and seemed to move more independently of one another than seemed normal.

Not often had I so carefully scrutinized a person who had been introduced so casually, but there was something about her that aroused my curiosity. Maybe I had been too long at the Yard. Maybe I saw in her the texture of personality that I once in a while came across at Guy's Hospital when I would comb the wards looking for the surgeon of record in a crime case. But perhaps I had inhaled too much Flanders wind and should just allow a Balkan woman to be, to escape my never-ending inquiry and move on. After all, I was on vacation.

I looked down into my cooling tea, where three leaves competed for my attention, all of them in Brownian motion. I then looked over to the MacCormicks. We entered into the usual get-to-know-you banter with some long and attentive looks between us. I quickly sensed that they had had interesting lives that a few moments of sincere conversation began to uncork. The MacCormicks did not disappoint.

Like many Canadians, they were full of warmth, conversation and homespun wisdom. James was an oil company executive, and Helen was a housewife, but a housewife with a deep and abiding interest in the world. I liked them immediately. James was a burly-armed, ebullient absorber of life. Helen was more retiring, but with a viper-like wit. Together, as became immediately clear, they were a life force. I was certain that in Calgary they would be in high demand at social functions, yet at the same time I could sense that there was more than the merely social about them. It was a lucky union. My own had not been graced by such luck.

Though I had said little about myself during our time at the table, they seemed interested in me and asked about my work. They indicated that one of their sons was a Royal Canadian Mounted Police detective in

Saskatchewan, so they understood much about the investigative mindset. James was very appealing. Full of fun on the surface, he was a natural listener and a very thoughtful man. Like all great businessmen, he was very attentive to moment-to-moment events. He was the sort of person who makes you instinctively consider your words carefully. Helen was full of laughter and fun, although she could pierce a piñata with a glare.

As I spoke with James and Helen, I learned that they were visiting Lark Farm on a personal mission. Like many Canadians from the Calgary region, they had lost relatives in WWI. At tables in that high plateau of Canada, talk still turns late on winter nights toward the immense loss that Alberta faced in the Great War, and many make the pilgrimage to the dead, even though they are separated now by generations.

When you trace back to that time, you can understand why. Canada was then a nation of only eight million people. In contrast, the British Empire in 1922 comprised 458 million people worldwide, and even Germany's population was 68 million during the war. Alberta, a western province, had a population of 500,000, most living in farming communities. The Canadians of that era and place were much removed from world politics. Yet, by virtue of their Commonwealth status with England, they were drawn into the Great War liked the hanged on the gallows when the trapdoor opens and gravity plays her part. Gone were the days of wheat and grain, the willows by the waters and the snow drifts shoulder high. The men were ported east on trains until trains could go no more. And then they were shipped. To Flanders. The farms of Alberta were rapidly depleted of them. The farms of Flanders absorbed them.

First in their thoughts, the MacCormicks explained, was the difficulty that families faced in coming to terms with the 'complete' loss of a loved one - that is, loss of life on a distant battlefield and with no remains to inter. This was especially poignant in Canada, whose citizens and troops were always considered to be "extras" and not front line troops in their own right, despite the fact that they too were on the front lines. It took time for the British in particular to realize the Canadians' fighting ferocity and formidable will. Who would have imagined it? Young men with no politics, tested only on farms, pitted against the greatest professional army in the world. Yet they became just angry and tactical enough to overwhelm their enemy at Passchendaele. They echeloned into death in enormous numbers, but always with considered progress. There was clearly something very special about the Canadians of that era.

Thousands of families in Alberta lost their sons, brothers, husbands and fathers. WWI remains a sacred event for the descendants of these families in Calgary, and James and Helen were examples of this spirit of remembrance. They were strong, diligent and honorable representatives of the region's commitment to its forebears.

As the group conversation died down, the three of us walked around the room, viewing the artwork on the walls and the memorabilia scattered on the shelves. There were black and white photos from the front, taken in 1917 during the constant August rains of that year. Men and horses could be seen floundering in the mud, and shell explosions could be seen in the distance. The mud actually seemed to grasp at their forms. In looking at the photos, one could almost hear the pelting rain and the explosions and feel the hatred and the despair.

There were also photos of the nearby city of Ypres, before and after its total destruction in 1915-1917. The massive and symbolic Lakenhalle (Cloth Hall), in particular, was savagely dissected by Big Bertha shells fired by the Germans from Houthulst Forest, eleven kilometers away. Ironically, the Lakenhalle initially became a victim of this shelling primarily because the wooden scaffolding that had been erected about its tower to restore it became the early and essential fodder for the fire that ultimately destroyed the building. In that year, seeing their beloved monuments and homes fall, the inhabitants left the city of Ypres *en masse* as refugees. Clusters of them moved south and east, some into the battleground of the Somme, where many eventually lost their lives in that unlivable traverse.

After the Armistice, despite thoughts that the fully destroyed Ypres should be preserved as a war memorial, its survivors returned to rebuild the city, timber by timber, back to its original glory. The magnitude of the German reparation funds that rebuilt the Lakenhalle may have ironically influenced the genesis of WWII, during which the people of Ypres also suffered.

Finally, there were photos on the walls of Lark farm as it appeared in 1913 and in 1917. While it was a tidy and prosperous settlement in the first photo, hardly a wall remained standing in the second. It wasn't hard to imagine the agony that those years had visited upon the very spot upon which I stood.

The artwork on the walls was exquisite. Men and women had taken the time to properly chart the carnage of war and the passage of time. The colors of the recent images were especially vivid by contrast with the black and white WWI images. The shelves of the meeting room held gas masks, bullets, artillery cartridges, medals and cloth unit badges.

One item stood out.

It was a small blue, white and gold striped cloth badge of apparently modern design. Helen, James and I were discussing its origin when Paula walked up to us and in an uncharacteristic whisper explained that it was her son Pieter's NATO Service Award. It was the only possession of his that the NATO force was able to find and return to them from Kosovo. A deathly quiet came over us until Paula broke the spell by saying, "It's all right. He is among his own, here." And she quietly turned and slipped away.

As she walked away, I looked out the window toward the barn and saw a slight, middle-aged man in overalls sitting oddly erect on the seat of his tractor as he passed by. I watched as he stopped, stepped down, detached a wagon, opened the great red barn doors and drove the tractor into the darkness. He was the same man I had seen in the field, earlier. Shortly afterward, he emerged, removed his cap and wiped his brow. He then grasped the shaft of the wagon and turned it about, directing it toward a pile of what appeared to be rusted cans. I watched as he dropped the back door of the wagon, exposing a number of similar canisters that he carefully placed with the rest. Then, he returned the wagon to the barn, closed the doors and headed for our building. Before he reached us, he carefully and extensively washed his hands using a nearby garbage hose. Then he dried his hands on his striped shirt and walked with a determined, short gait toward the door. When he entered, Paula hugged him and introduced us all to him as her husband, Thijs.

Thijs was a gentle but serious looking man. His clothes were old and dusty and when we shook hands, his was moist. His command of English was clearly not at as good as Paula's, but there was a directness and sincerity in his nature that required no translation. I immediately connected with him. He explained that he was pleased to have us all in their home and that he would be happy to assist us in any way that he could. At Paula's prompt, he gave us a brief review of the crops he was planting (corn and soybeans) and also told us what was in his wagon when he came in.

He said, "As I till the soil, I often uncover unexploded shells from the Great War. Today, I found eight unexploded shells in the far corner of the field. What was unusual about them was I couldn't be sure they weren't gas shells, so I was careful to wash carefully after handling them. We have a near-daily visit from the Belgian Bomb Disposal Battalion to take unexploded ordinance away. This week I've found many shells, and since the Battalion is on holiday until tomorrow, we have quite a little hill of munitions. You are welcome to take a stroll around the corner of the building to see them but please don't approach them too closely." Then, he smiled a half smile, put his head down slightly, grasped his cap and slipped quietly into the kitchen.

With that, I made my leave and walked over to the check-in desk, where Paula was efficiently processing the incoming guests. "Mr. Hendrick," she smiled. "You are the lucky one, as you get to stay in our Ell room. It is upstairs after you turn left at the end of the long hallway. The 'Ell' part is its beautiful extended bathroom. All of the other rooms are a bit more constrained. I hope that you enjoy it," she said as she handed over the keys.

Chapter 6: Reminiscence

Feeling like I had just received an unexpected airline upgrade, I mounted the stairs and found my way to my room at the end of the hallway. Along the way, I watched my head as I walked along the half A-frame roof with its imposing beams and noted the artwork on the left wall. One piece depicted World War I helmets in pencil and the others portrayed ardent mustachioed fighters sitting on a broken artillery piece, swathed in mud. I was pleased to tuck myself into my angle-beamed room, with its king-sized bed and well-appointed bathroom. It was far more luxurious than I had expected.

To celebrate my good fortune, I immediately opened my saddlebags and pulled out a bottle of *Bouchard et Fils Cotes du Rhone* that I had purchased in a small vintner's shop in Langemarck. I opened it and aired it by passing it back and forth between two sizable bathroom glasses. You know the kind: short, fat and unbreakable. We've all marveled at them, late in evenings, alone in hotel rooms. Wine clings to the sides of these glasses like latex paint on a wall. I then stripped off of my dusty biking jersey and shorts and shoes and socks. I poured a glass as I turned on the powerful shower in its tiled cage. I took a sip, set down my glass, entered the shower and reveled in the sting and the heat.

I was glad to be away from Scotland Yard, my failed marriage and, to a great extent, myself.

As I showered, I looked across the bathroom at my rumpled undershorts and remembered a special event in my life. I was twenty and had just finished the first phase of my criminal science education at Leicester after an aborted attempt at premedical studies (anatomy was the only subject that I had been able to master, ironically providing a good background for forensics work). I left for Barcelona on a vacation with friends at Easter time. We started by camping in Spain for several days on the Costa Brava and later wound up in a fifth floor walk-up hotel room on the Ramblas in Barcelona during *Semana Santa*. We all washed our dusty underwear in the sink and then hung it on the wrought iron railings that faced the Ramblas to dry in the hot spring air. Within 15 minutes, the Guardia Civil were at the door in force, truncheons a-ready. Amidst an excited babble of Catalan, we figured out that our underwear was viewed as an insult by the solemn religious processions, passing below. We removed our cottons, thanked the

Guardia for their reminder and held our breaths as they sternly departed. Generalisimo Franco's hand could still be felt, several years after his death.

The following day was Easter Sunday. I set out alone along the Ramblas as my camping friends left for England. I had another week of leisure on the continent ahead of me, and I was trying to sort out how to best enjoy it. I was wearing tumbledown black slacks and sandals and a baggy shirt and hadn't shaved. At ten, I sat down on an ornate wooden chair in a cafe that featured steaming mugs of coffee and enough room to spread out the newspaper I had snared from a former customer. I ordered a black coffee and a plain croissant. When I opened the pink Financial Times, a woman next to me asked if I was British.

I turned to her and said yes, I *was* British, She was an American, which I saw before she'd said a single word. She wore a Brooks Brothers blouse and a Talbot's sweater, the latter clinging to her curvy form. Of course, she wore khaki slacks to complete the American look. She was as attractive as she was friendly. I was suffused with that feeling one has when traveling abroad alone: am I really, truly making actual contact with another human being? So often when I traveled on the Continent in those years, I never spoke a word to anyone.

She leaned in and told me that she was traveling alone for the Easter holiday while in the middle of a year abroad. She was a music scholar from the University of Oklahoma, where she majored in the study of the cello. She'd grown up in Enid, Oklahoma, the single daughter of influential parents, her father running a railroad and her mother chairing the local art museum.

Her name was Bonnie.

We immediately moved our chairs together and engaged in a deeper conversation. She had vivid blue eyes and blonde hair that thinned to a fringe as it hung across her temples. Her lips curved in a cupid's bow, and her cheekbones were high. Some Indian heritage? I wondered. She talked with her hands and her face in synchrony, so that you could never interpret the story from just one or the other. On the table in front of her was a Mensa publication.

I admonished myself for having expected a certain American shallowness, for she was very intelligent. I wondered why a woman like this was alone in Barcelona on Easter Sunday. Then I looked at my garb and wondered why she was speaking to me at all. She allayed that concern by saying that she had a brother like me and would never know why we men dressed as we did. But she had grown to accept it.

Then she said the unthinkable. She asked if I would attend Mass with her.

Now, I had lost my faith in God about twenty years before I was born, so this came as a shock. In one fell swoop, she had negated both free sex, and the free afternoon and early drinking I had been counting on. But hope never dies, so I perked up in my chair and said:

"Of course! I'd love to!"

She refused to let me pay the bill, afterward patted her thin wallet into a protected pocket and led me on my way to the *Catedral de la Santa Creu* for the noontime high mass.

What a picture we two made as we slithered through ardent groups of overdressed Catalans into the Cathedral to find a cleft in the crowd from which to watch the priests and to inhale the low-lying incense cloud that flowed our way. In the end, I was but an ellipse of black and grey and stubble in the midst of flowery dresses, brilliant shoes and an adjacent sliver of Talbots and Brooks Brothers.

But it was fabulous to be there.

When the Mass ended, the real festivities began. The populace squeezed from the Cathedral in family units. Once in its courtyard, they began dancing, all as one. Little children, parents, and grandparents leaped to the beat of an impromptu band as others watched, clapping. Bonnie and I were tempted to join in, but I felt we could only undo the spell we were witnessing. It went on for hours and gave me a sense of the Catalan as no event has ever done since.

Bonnie and I then spent the day climbing the promontory south of Barcelona and filled the late afternoon viewing families strolling distant streets and the always-interesting affairs of the harbor and the open sea. We dined there on octopus, thick crusts of bread, peppers in olive oil and a cheese whose aroma befit some dark, wheat-choked plain. We drank two bottles of *Rioja* and kissed for longer and longer periods. We returned through darks streets to her rooming house, where a stern, buxom chaperone warned me against entering by placing her ample form in the small doorway.

While warding off the chaperone for a moment, Bonnie penned and then handed me a note and bade me good-bye. As the chaperone listened, she said that she would be leaving in the morning on a very early train, nodding subtly to the note in my hand as she spoke. After completing our good-byes, I returned to my nearby hotel, sat on the bed under the single lamp and read her note:

"Dear Nigel - I am living this year in Lyon in the apartment of a very prominent vintner. The family is in their vacation home in Nice for the next month. Please come and visit me on your way home.

Yours,
Bonnie"

She had included the address and phone number on the back.

The following Friday, she was waiting for me at the Statue de la Republique on the Place Carnot, adjacent to the Gare de Lyon-Perrache. It was springtime and warm and in the Second Arrondissement of Lyon, the sun was shining and the air was lively. She wore light gray slacks and a blouse of cerulean blue. Her long hair was shifting here and there in the light wind as I approached, and she smiled and held out her arms. After we embraced, she asked me if I would like to sit for a bit at one of the nearby cafes and I thought it was an excellent idea. On the southeastern side of the Place, a cafe known locally as *The Zephyr* was just opening for its afternoon offerings. Bonnie ordered a Kir and I a Kronenbourg. We toasted one another.

As we drank, we looked out at the Place Carnot, and she said, "Carnot was an exemplary Frenchman of the Revolution. He was able to maintain honorable positions before, during and after the Revolution and was embraced by Napoleon. Only in later years did he run afoul of politics and then had to escape to Poland and Prussia. He died in Magdeburg, Germany, but is now interred in the Pantheon in Paris. He was the ultimate military and civil organizer and is well known in engineering circles for his description of the Carnot Engine - the most efficient engine that can live within the Laws of Thermodynamics."

She knew so much!   I asked, "Bonnie, how do you know so much about Carnot?"

Blushing, she pulled from her breast pocket a small brochure that she had obtained from the Visitor's Center a few yards away and handed it to me. "You were late, and I like to read." She smiled.

It was all right there, on Page One.

We laughed and finished our drinks and she said "Come on, I need to show you something special." I pulled my backpack on and stepped behind her as she entered a bus that took us to *Vieux Lyon*, on the west bank of the Saone, high on a hill. As we exited the bus, she entered what appeared to be a slit in a nearby wall. Down a ramp we went in near darkness, hearing nothing but dripping on cement as went. Finally, we stood on a nearly level platform in what was a narrow tunnel with an arched roof and periodic lighting. "Welcome to Fourviere Hill and the Traboules," she said, sweeping her arms upward. "These were the conduits through which the Canuts - the silk workers - would bring their wares to waiting barges on the Saone River." Then, she stopped speaking, leaned into me, and kissed me, a hint of Kir on her breath. "Come on," she said, "Let's do some exploring."

We spent the better part of the next hour following underground passages, mostly alone but once in awhile standing hard against the wall to allow usually solitary Lyonnais to pass. Sometimes, we would emerge into courtyards, sometime into storage areas, sometimes into open air. The Traboules seemed to be endless. Finally, at a three-point intersection of the Traboules, she said, "Let's go this way."

In moments, we were standing amidst an open market on the Rue Saint-Georges, and Bonnie was bartering in French with a seller of chickens. She paid for a small chicken, produced from her purse a burlap sack, and deposited the chicken within. She then accosted a man nearby whose sign read "Legumes" and came away with potatoes, parsley and onions. Finally, she bought a long, thin baguette and two bottles of *Cotes du Rhone* and said, "Come on, Nigel, we have some walking to do."

And walk we did, she with her burlap sack draped over one arm, tethered by the other and I with my backpack, laden with unspeakably soiled clothing. The thing was heavy and I wished that I had stashed it at the railroad station. Over the Pont Bonaparte we walked, then to Place Bellecour, where we rested among the trees, watched the pigeons and ate lemon ice to cool us. After our rest, we walked down the streets of Presqu'ile, finally turning a corner onto the rue Antoine de Saint-Exupery, where the famous aviator/writer was born. As we walked past his boyhood home, Bonnie took a key from her pocket and ascended three short steps to the front door of the building next door, opened it and invited me in.

The hallway was wide, made of stone, and it was dark and cool. We walked up three flights to a landing facing a massive wooden door, which she opened. On its opposite side, a red velvet rug was hung to absorb hallway sounds. As I entered the apartment, I noticed that it held very little furniture and only the occasional small throw rug. The bookshelves were full of old French classics and on the tables, beautiful books containing watercolor scenes of Aix en Provence, Brittany and Paris were open. As we went to the kitchen, I noticed that the only mechanical device (other than stove and refrigerator) was a rather old electric can opener.

"Bonnie," I asked "Is this really the apartment of a wealthy French vintner?" "Yes," she replied. "Why do you ask?"

I took a moment before responding, then said: "But they seem to live so sparingly."

She smiled and informed me that only the *nouveau riche* show ostentation in Lyon. The firm of *Brevard et Fils* was well known and respected as a producer of Burgundy wine and yes, the family was exceptionally wealthy. "I was invited to stay with them this year because Monsieur Brevard is a friend of my father's. Come open the wine and let it breathe for a second or two and pour me a glass." She looked at me directly, smiled and said, "I'm quite thirsty, you know."

I complied, as she emptied the burlap sack and set the items on the counter. Soon she had the oven on and was washing and drying the chicken. As she did, she mentioned "So we are not in the apartment next to the birthplace of Saint-Exupery by accident, you know." I asked her for clarification between sips of wine and she replied;

"Monsieur Brevard worships him as an historical figure and bought this apartment at a steep price simply to be close to his memory." She went on "As a young man, Monsieur Brevard was touched by Saint-Exupery's book *'The Little Prince'* which is about a young boy who appears to the survivor of a desert airplane crash and asks that the pilot draw him a sheep for him to take back to his home, the Asteroid B-612."

I listened intently as she continued "Monsieur Brevard was but a little boy who became distraught when Saint-Exupery was lost without a trace while flying a warplane over the Mediterranean Sea in 1944." Then she paused and said "Now let me show you the unique way that Monsieur Brevard has memorialized Saint-Exupery. Look, for example, at the labels of the wine bottles." Both, I noticed, were Brevard wines. "Look in the lower right hand corner of each and tell me what you see." I did so and initially could not make out anything of interest when suddenly, a nearly holographic image that read B-612 danced before my eyes and then was gone. When I tried to elicit it again, I could not. "Amazing," I thought, as I looked up to Bonnie, my mouth ajar.

"It's a remarkable way to remember the lost, isn't it?" Bonnie said.

Just then, the oven preheating timer beeped and Bonnie began preparing the chicken in earnest. First she coated it inside and out with salt, pepper and freshly chopped parsley, some of which she inserted under the skin, through tiny incisions. Then, she took a lemon from the refrigerator, sliced it into three pieces and inserted each into the cavity of the chicken. Finally, she coated her hands with olive oil and patted the bird inside and out before placing it in a baking tray, breast-side up. She inserted it into the oven and closed the door.

We chatted idly as the chicken cooked, which warmed the kitchen and made a beautiful aroma that augmented our hunger. Bonnie had me peel the potatoes, which she sliced into rounds, just as she had done with the onions. She added butter and oil to a frying pan and added the potatoes and onions, followed by salt and pepper. Turning them frequently she sang a song in French that included the words "Potatoes Lyonnais," all the while enjoying wholesale quaffs from her glass, her face pink and beaming. When they were just about cooked, she threw in a handful of chopped parsley with a firmly stated "Voila," then stirred the parsley throughout the mixture. She left the warm potatoes in the pan as she withdrew the finished chicken from the oven. She wrapped it in foil for ten minutes, then set it on a resting plateau and said, "Nigel, do you carve?"

I did.

Soon, we had all we needed before us for a delightful repast. We sat at a modest wooden table and Bonnie brought out utensils that had clearly been used for a century or more. As I waited for her to come to the table, I looked at the forks, spoons and knives. They each had a tarnished old look about them but once in awhile, I thought I saw an electronic B-612 emit from them. I knew it was the wine, but the story was that powerful.

Bonnie and I ate this simple food in a fever of joy.

I don't ever think I have ever had a chicken that was so moist and flavorful. The Brevard wines were intoxicating, so much so that when I completed my meal, I needed to retire to the large chair with the ottoman in the family room. No pies, no glaces were needed. This Brevard wine and Bonnie's cooking were enough: narcosis set in. And so I slept peacefully until whatever hour I awoke. It was after dawn.

When I sat up, the apartment was still. I walked about. There were no dishes in the sink. There was no garbage in the bag. There were no potato peelings and no onion skins. In fact, there was nothing to indicate that we had ever eaten here. I also noticed that the books of watercolors that had lain on the tables were closed and shelved.

And there was no Bonnie.

I walked to the rug that held the hallway sounds back and found a note pinned to it that read, "Please lock the door when you leave." And no more.

Think about your reaction under these circumstances. So many questions! Yet I had the good sense to take a shower in the old bathroom, get dressed, perplexed as could be, and leave. Over the next months and years, I would write to the Brevards, but I never received a response. Finally, I called, and a woman answered. I could hear an electric can opener operating in the background. "No," she said, "We have never had an American visitor stay with us here." With that, she hung up the phone, and I let Bonnie go.

Now in my luxury shower on Lark Farm, there was something about remembering that experience that reset me, that made me ready for the future, challenged though it might be. My lost relationship. My ex-wife never speaking to me. It seems that I needed a little more wine, so I stepped out of the shower, dried off and partook.

The Ell room had a south-facing window with a nook. Sitting in this slight alcove, I was able to enjoy the warmth of the sun, which at that time of year remained high in the sky. As I sat there, I reflected on how being at Lark Farm and in this Flemish battlefield focused my thoughts on episodes of inconsolable loss. Try as I might to force my thoughts to match the weather, I could not.

In a brief reverie there, I was thrown back to the year I completed my University studies. I took a brief trip to Ireland, explored Dublin and walked the circumferential cliff walk at cool and misty Howth Head, far above the Irish Sea. I recalled being alone and pensive. Howth Head does that to one. I imagined those sailors whose ships were sunk in adjacent waters by U-Boats that could be seen surfacing from its heights. The sailors swimming amidst the wreckage were too close to shore to lose hope but too far from shore in that cold and rough sea to survive.

That's the Irish Sea.

At the end of my walk, I sat in a nearby pub beneath a portrait of a young man in military attire. Seeing my interest in the portrait, the proprietor exclaimed that it was of his grandfather. A physicist at Trinity College in his precocious early adulthood, his grandfather was on the verge of discovering a new principle of matter when he volunteered for service with the British Expeditionary Force in 1914 and was lost within a day of service at Wytschaete. He, like many others of his rank that day, had simply vanished.

Looking out from my Lark Farm alcove, I finished my bottle of wine. I muddled forward and dressed myself in evening garb that could only be considered Expeditionary Force Luxe. Khaki pants, light shirt and a green overcoat. With these clothes, I could have fit into any off-duty army in the world. I was attired to ride and hoped to be able to enjoy the evening, despite my reminiscences.

I went downstairs and outside. I retrieved Max Mobilier from the garage and looked it over. Once you have ridden a bike a bit, you see it more fully. Max was a remarkable piece of Belgian engineering. Strong struts and tubes, red as could be, its structure spoke not of speed but of substance. Moreover, its seat spoke of comfort. Like the latter WWI tanks, Max Mobilier was designed for strength and momentum. Unlike the tanks, though, Max was primarily designed for Flanderian cycling purposes - to maintain momentum through gusts of wind. Having ridden 70 km from Ghent that day in high winds, I knew the value of my machine. I climbed on board and started my ride toward Passchendaele and the pleasures of *De Salient*, the bar of reunion where I would once again meet Wouter Deert for a fine Belgian beer or two.

The sun was still one quarter high when I set my foot on Max's right pedal. After a few gravelly, wine-soaked misturns, I was underway. Unlike the day's long previous ride into head winds, this early evening bike-stroll felt mellow. Though my forearms and my behind could feel that they had been ridden hard earlier, there was something about the mild discomfort that made the resumed ride seem purposeful. As I left the farmyard, a group of cats crossed the road in front of me, aloof and full of stealth. I turned toward the east and made the proper series of left and right turns on narrow, paved lanes that ultimately delivered me past strawberry farms and fallow fields to the main local road, 's Graventafelstraat.

When on the way to Passchendaele from the southwest, 's Graventafelstraat forms the inner arc of a two-rimmed china plate, the outer rim provided by the town of Passchendaele, itself. As I headed north on 's Graventafelstraat, slowly expanding my exertion to surmount the very mild rise toward Passchendaele, I stopped and realized that I was cycling on the exact place where the slaughter of the Canadians had taken place in the Third Battle of Ypres. Halfway to Passchendaele was no place to be in the summer and autumn of 1917. Right here they fought bravely and died horribly and were swallowed up whole.

From here I could see the sun from a different vantage point. Its rays were weakening, and a cloudbank began to interfere with its warmth as it sank slowly away. But it still illuminated many sites of critical interest - the steeple of the Church in Passchendaele, the blockish Canadian Memorial at the breakthrough point at the end of Canadalaan Avenue, the distant, very tall tower dedicated to the Canadians at Vancouver Corner to the west, the old windmill in the nearby west that the Germans used as an observation point while gassing Canadian troops, the massive Tyne Cot Cemetery to the southeast and finally, to the immediate west side of the road two hundred meters hence, the New British Commonwealth Cemetery.

It only took only a little cajoling of Max on the pedals to reach the cemetery, as traffic was minimal. I noticed as I slowed to stop, that the Brits from the B&B were just departing, having made their pilgrimages to relatives there.

When you enter a British Commonwealth cemetery on a bicycle, your first concern is where to put it. The cemeteries have no bike racks and seem so sacred that you dare not sully their entrances even with a craft as sublime as Max. So I found a highway sign nearby and leaned Max against it, as if tying a beloved dog to a stump for a bit, watching over my shoulder even as I went forth. All alone, I entered the white marble arch and iron gates of the cemetery. Several thousand soldiers are buried there, most having been relocated after the war at one time or another. The tombstones are all identical in size and shape and are in military lines.

They are profoundly touching.

The great majority of the tombstones exhibit the inscription *"A Soldier of the Great War,"* indicating that the remains that were interred were simply unidentifiable other than to be known to have been human. Some of the tombstones, however, were carved with a name or simply a rank. There were Londoners, Yorkshiremen, New Zealanders, Australians, Canadians and sundry others from the far reaches of the British Empire.

Men came from families throughout the world and in a large fraction of cases were never heard from again. When walking the length of the New British Cemetery, I noticed that I had misperceived its extent. About two-thirds of the way into the cemetery, it takes about a two-meter dip down a hill and in an almost grave like depression bears another thousand tombstones. In between the stones, flowers grow, some of them blood-red poppies that flutter in their characteristically fragile way in the wind.

When walking out of the cemetery to the right side gate, I found a metal door in the wall that covered a niche in the marble and a modern, bound notebook. Like a B&B guestbook, it was filled with comments from visitors from around the world. Many were simply congratulatory of the maintenance of the site and its beauty but some reached deeper. Three touched me:

"Tom was a boy when we sent him here. He became a man too quickly and then he chose God over us."

"We know of Axel only as a great-great granduncle but we recall great grandmother's inexhaustible pain and her life of waiting for him to return to her."

"I lost no relatives in the Great War but lost a daughter to aught knows what...for onwards of twelve years now and no sign.."

I really did need to get on and meet with Wouter.

Yet I was so impressed by this site and these reminiscences that I stood with my bike helmet under my arm and my ridiculous shorts on my waist and tried to fully absorb what this sacrifice was all about. I sheltered myself in the right gate with its hard marble bench as I came to tears, thinking how all of these small, dedicated people from around the world became noble through their sacrifice at the hands of powerful and probably misguided leaders.

It took me a bit of time to compose myself and get to the point at which I could blame the Flanders wind for the redness of my face and for the swelling around my eyes once I reunited with Wouter.

Chapter 7: Passchendaele

No one else visited the New British Commonwealth Cemetery before I left, so I was alone in low light when I bade it farewell, looking deeply first west into the sky of the Allied Powers and then east, toward Passchendaele, the sky of the German invader. I turned on Max's front and rear lights as I cycled quickly north on 's Graventafelstraat to the T-junction with Vierde Regiment Karabiniersstraat, upon whose right turn I climbed the final easy meters into town.

Like many places that have been tragically afflicted with total warfare, Passchendaele seemed on its limited outskirts to be utterly unaffected by its unlucky history. Small row houses buttressed one another up the gentle hill into town. Wide walkways belied the perils of entry into the town in 1917. At the top of the hill, the Church stood prominently, squarish in its base. I had wanted to take a quick look inside, as its north-facing stained glass window was purported to be so special. It was not to happen, though: a red-flower-bedecked hearse stood outside and a query to an onlooker revealed that the evening funeral of the town's most revered surgeon was underway. Before leaving, I took time to view the ghastly array of black and white local family tombstones in the adjacent Churchyard.

They were an odd lot, some a display of twisted black metal symbolic forms and others with seemingly recent photos of long dead relatives taped to concrete. There is a visibility to death in that Church courtyard that you rarely see in other small towns. It is unsettling. It may be that the local population has had their overall view of death distorted so much by virtue of their wartime legacy that the usual patterns of death and remembrance have been disrupted. Passchendaelians seem determined to preserve a connection with their long dead, even if it diminishes the present.

It was with these sad thoughts that I pedaled my way half a block back down Vierde Regiment Karabienersstraat to its junction with Grenadiersstraat, where I turned left and after a short distance met a most welcome site, the pub/hotel *De Salient*. Built between several homes of limited height, *De Salient* stood forth with authority. Although completely rebuilt after WWI, *De Salient* had a nineteenth century look. Constructed of red brick with contrasting white border stones, its roof was hidden by a terraced building face and was crested by a spire bearing a half moon whose arc tilted toward the east. Small, deep-set windows punctuated its face, each gripping a flower box in which lush red poppies grew in thick sets. The building was set diagonally to the prevailing wind and this fostered swirling of the wind that threw the poppies first one way then the other, even in the calmest air. The place was a statement: it was alive. From within, I could hear raucous locals, certainly enjoying their pints of Duvel and Chimay beer, in addition to the benighted local Passendale ale.

I locked my bike against a tree deep in the adjacent yard, where a shawled elderly woman was working in a garden. Her small gloved hands were softly working a small trowel around two objects in the dirt. Curious, I came closer to see what was interesting her. She looked over at me and with a wrinkled smile pulled a small bone from the loam, a tarsal bone, I knew from my forensic osteology days. She set it in a small pile with similar others, next to which lay a small shell of the type used to distribute mustard gas. She spoke English and told me that even such a pleasure as gardening had to be approached carefully in Flanders. She then went to a nearby house to report her findings to both the Graves Commission and the Bomb Disposal Battalion for later retrieval.

When I entered *De Salient*, I was immediately struck by its dark and sinister interior.

It was designed to give the impression that you were entering a trench that took a circuitous path through the building. The narrow halls were sandbagged and slatted, all in grey tones. Light came only obliquely from above, where strands of barbed wire hung here and there. The walkway was made of slightly raised, framed boards and side rooms burst from the hallway at odd angles and at odd heights. In each, there were tables with candles burning, shedding faint light on framed images of old Passchendaele, infantry and broken trees and buildings. By contrast, in each of the side rooms, lively fellows were sipping their beers from glasses that were especially designed for each type of beer they were enjoying. The elliptical glass holding Passendale beer, for example, stood in stark contrast to the full-bellied glass that held Chimay. The men were laughing and telling tales and seemed oblivious to me as I passed. A waiter wearing fatigues squeezed past me with a full tray of beer, bringing reinforcements to the front.

As I walked along, I saw a bright light ahead as the structure opened up into a full room. It was the bar. Along the walls were shelves made from what looked like soldiers' cots. They were brimming with liquor bottles. The top of the bar itself was covered with topographical maps, showing placements of army divisions, weapons depots and lines of advance. They were decoupaged in place with thick, church pew varnish that could withstand the dew from the heartiest mug. Behind, a fire was roaring in a dugout area surrounded by a host of tables at which several couples were dining on frites and Flemish stew.

The bartender wore a Canadian General's uniform and sported a handlebar mustache. He was ruddy-faced and friendly. "What can I pour for you?" he asked.

"I'll try a Passendale Ale," I replied, and then asked him if he had seen Wouter Deert on the premises.

As he passed my beer down the bar to me he glowed with a smile and with a directional flourish of his arm said, "Wouter's in the back - and you must be Nigel.

He's expecting you."

With my beer in hand, I took a deep sip and then cradled it for the walk. I noticed that weapons were featured in each of the alcoves of the bar. In one room, there were rifles on the wall. In another, bayonets. As I ambled toward the back room, I not only looked forward to meeting Wouter but also to seeing why he had chosen this place for us to meet.

Then I was there. At the end of a long dark grey hallway, I entered a square room that held a large planning table, surrounded by circumferential shell casings on racks. A sizable, centrally placed bottle of dark Belgian beer was positioned between an imposing, black-haired, strongly built man and me: my old friend, Wouter. Two deep-troughed glasses sat a meter apart on the table. As I entered the room, he poured them full for each of us with a European elegance and then palmed the two drinks together as if to say that the Channel no longer separated us. I downed the remains of my Passendale as he thrust a mug toward me.

I gave Wouter a big hug, trying my best not to spill the beer on our shirts. He was a substantial man, not only in his personal heft but also in his personality. His hair, thrown to the right across his forehead, was wire-like on his very large head. Yet his smile was so warm that his more imposing features were effectively brought into line behind an intelligent Belgian self-deprecation.

As in all meetings of old friends after years, two conversations initially take place simultaneously, the external and the internal, the latter adapting rapidly to the changes in one another's appearances and circumstances until finally the two conversations converge and comfort is once again felt. This happened without effort for each of us. Wouter had changed but little.

We sat down in this equivalent of a General's quarters at the front, toasted peace together and immediately began to talk. As Wouter spoke, he folded and unfolded his magnificent hands around his beer glass, the table's edge and one another. We spoke sadly about our wives and reminisced about the times when we had all shared walks in Hyde Park and picnics in Greenwich. We also spoke of our work together at the Yard and especially how Wouter's experiences there had prepared him for a prominent forensic role in Belgium.

He said, "Recall that in the nineties we were the first in England to experiment with the application of the Polymerase Chain Reaction and Gene Expression Microarrays in analyzing nucleotide patterns at crime scenes. No one believed that we could crack that Docklands case of human trafficking until we revealed the data match between the DNA samples of the lost Estonian girls and the DNA found in the shipping containers. That was when I became convinced we needed to have similar facilities here in Belgium. It took a little time and work, including many visits to the European Union headquarters in Brussels, but ultimately I was able to build the Center for Molecular Forensics in Moorslede, just a few kilometers east of here. We now employ twenty technicians and perform all of the molecular forensics work in Belgium and the Netherlands. All because of your invitation to spend that sabbatical year at the Yard, Nigel."

"And because of your successful demonstration of these capabilities in London, we have greatly expanded our staff and equipment since then," I replied, "Many of our Inspectors speak of how you persistently introduced the new technology with little fanfare but great success."

"A Belgian attribute, Nigel." He smiled wryly as he poured us more beer and proffered a bowl of very brown bread, already buttered. "I think you would be interested in some of the things that we have learned, working here. As you know, we toil in the midst of one of the most lethal battlefields on earth. Our soil is filled with the remains of men from countries all over the world, thanks to the British and German empires' contributions to the war. Consequently, whenever we retrieve a forensic sample from the soil, there is always a question regarding the age and origin of the human DNA we find.

"Recent studies have indicated that DNA in the soil initially degrades quickly but then breaks apart rather steadily over perhaps hundreds of years. This varies between sites, because it appears that wetter and more acidic terrain is more destructive to DNA. However, even in these sites, we find a persistence of fragments that can be used to verify human remains. Ironically, the degradation of different DNA types over time make it seem that we are more alike as persons and nations than would have been the case if we had measured the shed DNA initially. This is why there has been a highly variable ability to conclusively identify WWI dead as individuals. But we have a good idea of the nation of origin and can reliably identify remains as human."

"One important discovery we have made is that despite the massive Flanderian backdrop of multinational soil-bound DNA, we can almost always subtract that signal away from a new DNA signal, which is far more intact."

We sipped our beer, ate sandwiches of cheese and eel and simply enjoyed being together. As always, Wouter was scientifically way ahead of me. He already understood the implications of this new technology for his special landscape. And this had become particularly important in Passchendaele the week before, when he had been able to differentiate the DNA of a missing Spanish girl in the backyard soil of a home in a rural district where she had briefly lain in a shallow grave, though in the companionship of perhaps hundreds of lost German and Canadian soldiers.

"Wouter," I said, in a willful attempt to change the subject, "What are you doing with yourself in your spare time?"

He laughed. "Nigel, you assume that I have any free time as Chief of Police in Passchendaele and Head of the Center?"

"Yes," I said. "I know how clever you can be with time."

He nodded, beaten, smiled and said, "Well, you know how I have always loved to fish." I immediately imagined that Wouter had found a way to purchase a boat and drift about in the nearby and elegant Netherlands waters, but he quickly retorted "And I was always jealous of your fly fishing ability. I remember the time that you and I took a beat on the Test and tried the dry flies on rising fish in the chalk waters. I also remember that night in the Mayfly Inn when you showed me how to tie even the tiniest flies, even when under the influence of a sodden artillery barrage of single malts. I left that night determined to be able to do the same, though I never let that on to you."

"When I returned to Belgium, one thing became clear: in the main, our low elevation could never support the well-oxygenated running water that trout require, except perhaps in the Ardennes. As a result, I learned to tie flies and fish for the local populations. Yes, I bought all of the equipment and materials for fly tying, but I had to modify my expectations and techniques. I went out and bought a seven-weight rod and began fishing the Belgian canals in their subsurface waters. I would do this from the shore, even as large barges were passing by. To my surprise, I began catching trophy-sized carp. I know such fish would not interest you, but catching them is an appreciated skill here. So I also learned to tie flies for carp and they work very well. Over the years, I have also adapted these flies to tell stories. And one of the stories they tell is yours."

With that, he pulled three full-sized flies from his pocket and displayed them on the table in front of me.

"This one," he said, "Commemorates your origins. It is composed of the colors of the Hendrick family coat of arms. Note the red wing, the grey abdomen, the black thorax and the tail of flesh." I was astounded. Then he said... "And the second commemorates your tenure at the Yard." He lay before me a Silver Ghost pattern composed entirely of white and grey. A beautiful streamer. "The last," he said, " Is to commemorate your pursuit of the future." He laid before me a fly colored entirely in crimson: wing, thorax, abdomen, rib and tail.

I asked, "What does this signify?"

He responded "I tied this just today when one of my officers who passed you en route from Bruges to Lark Farm described your bicycle, a Max Mobilier, to me. With this cycling trip, you are taking the first step into your future. I am very pleased for you. I hope that you enjoy your tour of Flanders," he said, and smiled broadly.

Wouter, that Belgian prescient, had me, once again. It was true: I had been thinking of the next phase in my life, now that my return home was sure to be lonesome. I pocketed the flies gratefully. He filled my glass often.

The evening pleasantly wore on until finally he said, smiling, as we arose, "Come on, Nigel, after these multiple beers you will need a police escort back to Lark Farm. Unfortunately, our Belgian patrol cars are too small to accept your bike, so just get on it and follow closely behind my rear running lights. There's no need to alert the populace to your condition with the siren and flashers, he smiled."

So I went back deep into the garden, fumbled with my padlock and teetered unskillfully through the garden stones to the parking lot where Wouter sat in his patrol car, in charge. I followed him back down Vierde Regiment Karabiniersstraat to 's Graventafelstraat and then through the winding lanes to Lark Farm.

As we approached, I thought I saw a fleeting shadow in the nearby right-side farmyard, but then again, Belgian beer is strong. I met Wouter at the window of his patrol car and said goodnight. I told him I'd be back in touch after sightseeing tomorrow, and I thanked him for those thoughtful flies, which I patted in my right pocket to be sure they were there. Then he was gone in a rush of engine noise in the starlit Flanders night.

I steered Max Mobilier to the safety of the barn, entered the B&B with my key and sauntered up the wooden stairs and down the long hall to the Ell room, where I fell, clothed, onto my bed. My last waking thought was that Wouter and I had never made it to dinner in Poelcapelle, after all.

Chapter 8. Canadalaan

When I awoke, I was lying sideways on the bed, with all my clothes on. It was 2 am. The hour of forgiveness. At that hour, if you get your clothes off and get back into bed within five minutes, you are bound to enjoy a sound sleep until morning. So I complied, despite my mature age and the prickly flies in my pocket. As I lay back down, the soft sound of the front door latch downstairs reached my ears through the otherwise completely still night. Had I been completely sober, I would have wondered who might be stirring on the farm at this odd hour. Perhaps a very late arrival or just an attentive Thijs checking on the livestock? Or maybe the ghost stories that were part of the *"Untold Tales"* were true and that men who had died on these grounds were stirring, exploring… There was one Canadian Corporal in particular who had come from a farm near Red Deer, Alberta, who, absent both his arms, was said to have returned to his unit several times after death to offer tea to his colleagues. I pondered this for a moment, and then sleep extinguished all active thought. When I woke in the morning, I had forgotten about the door latch entirely.

My plan for the day was to ride Max to as many of the Great War sites in Flanders as I could. There was so much to see, and I was not sure of my endurance. To reach my lofty goal, I would need a good breakfast.

Paula did not disappoint.

One of the niceties of travel in Europe is the full breakfast that is often included in the hospitality tariff. As one might have expected of a perfectionist like Paula, her breakfast buffet table was cornucopic in its excesses. At one end of the long meeting table lay the juices - orange, tomato, grapefruit, cranberry and pomegranate. All of them were offered in crystal decanters immersed in crushed and glistening ice. Next lay the eggs, soft boiled, fried and scrambled, all gently warmed, followed by cold cuts and cheese slices and Brie and Camembert on little warming tables next to six or seven types of thick crusted rolls that covered the spectrum from dark to light, from rustic artisanal to mainstream loaves. Then gravlax lay in full display, coated with perpendicular ferns of dill, chilling on a special plate with cream cheese near a cracker barrel. Cereals of all varieties were suspended within dispensers next to the milk, cream, teas and coffees. Fruit of many types was interspersed everywhere, as were jams and marmalades and butter pads.

I saw Marijke setting out an array of small herring that required peeling and preparation with a sauce at the table. I was astonished at her dexterity. Heads and tails and fish skin flew into a waste bowl. Then she sliced the herring into uniform tangential disks that she immediately coated with capers and sour cream. It was a performance worthy of the stage.

I loaded and carried two full plates back to a side table at which the MacCormicks were just beginning to eat their breakfasts and asked if I could join them. They were pleased to have me and I was pleased to notice that they had two full plates apiece, too. These good-natured Canadians, James and Helen, were growing on me. I also noticed that they each had two cups of coffee! " Like a good Brit, I ambled off to retrieve a little pot of tea and then realized that I would probably consume two cups, too - and perhaps more.

In the course of our conversation, they told me that last evening they had taken the short drive to Poelcapelle and had eaten in the very restaurant - *The Arrow* - that Wouter had recommended to me the day before. They were delighted with their experience there. The restaurant was rather modern and was run by a young married couple that lived upstairs from the restaurant. James and Helen mentioned that the unusual thing about the restaurant was that it had an atmosphere akin to restaurants in Toronto or New York, yet it was located in a tiny town in Flanders. James went on and on about his *Rabbit Tagliatelle with Arugula,* and Helen stressed her good fortune with the *Red Pepper Bisque* and *Chicken Confit over Wild Rice.* The wine list was substantial and the Ports and desserts were first class. These Canadians were indeed hearty eaters!

How they were able to eat so soon again, however, was a mystery to me. While sturdy in appearance, they were not obese. They were clearly active types.

I commented on their excellent appetites, and smiled. They did the same and asked me about my night. I told them about my long friendship with Wouter and about the very unusual pub/hotel *De Salient.* They were intrigued and wished that they could see it (and perhaps even stay there) but indicated that they would be on their way that day after doing some local sightseeing before making their pilgrimage to the Menin Gate that evening. They would be staying at the *Ambergris Hotel* in Ypres afterward. The following morning, they planned to take a drive to Dunquerque and then down the coast to the WWII landing sites in Normandy before enjoying a little vacation in Paris. Then, they would head home to Calgary.

I asked them what places they planned to visit today and they outlined a series of destinations much like my own, the only difference being that I would be seeing these sights on bicycle and they would be seeing them by car. Thinking that it might be nice to find one another later to compare notes on our experiences, I asked them if we might have lunch together somewhere reasonably close to a mutually attractive historic site. They immediately agreed to this and suggested a return to *The Arrow* in Poelcapelle.

Helen said "That would be the most convenient for us since we need to stop by there anyway - I think I lost my cell phone in the sofa seat where we dined last night. They don't open until noon, so we will just plan our driving tour to reach Poelcapelle about then. The restaurant is very close to the Canadian monument at Vancouver Corner, too." I consulted my map and agreed that a meeting at *The Arrow* would be ideal. Then, I realized that my cycling speed might be unpredictable so I said "While this breakfast has given me great strength, it may be best to trade our cell phone numbers in case I have overestimated my impression of my cycling capability." We all laughed and James wrote down his number for me. I wrote mine down for him, too. Armed with connectivity, we completed our meals and departed from the dining room.

As I walked past the kitchen, I heard Thijs speaking with Marijke about a large shell that he had discovered the day before. "Marijke, I will be plowing in the far field today. Paula has left word with the Bomb Disposal Battalion, and I would like to be present when they finally unearth the Big Bertha shell, just to keep everyone at a distance. It is a massive, very destructive shell, nothing like the 'soup cans' that I normally unearth while plowing. I will not be able to hear a phone call over the sound of the tractor but will keep watch for your usual signal when I am needed. Just wave your arms at the back door when you know the Battalion is coming and I will stop and call you to establish the time to come in and see the final retrieval." "Yes, sir, I will," she said, in broken English, her dark eyes never leaving his. Her delicate hands gripped the back of a kitchen chair, a little too firmly, I thought. Perhaps her papers were not completely in order, I imagined. Then again, that may once again have just been the Scotland Yard in me. And I was clearly trying to expunge that, during this vacation.

I went upstairs to the Ell room, sorry to be missing the spectacle of the removal of the Big Bertha shell. After dressing in my highly unflattering cycling garb, I packed my saddlebags with my clothes and maps as well as water, juices and energy bars and set off down the hallway toward the stairs. As I passed the MacCormicks' open door, I saw them searching about their room to pack the last of their belongings, said my goodbyes and headed down the stairs to the front door. As I passed the breakfast room, Paula came out and effusively hugged me and wished me well on my tour. After I paid my bill, she said, "We look forward to having you back again sometime and hearing all about your travels, Nigel." I promised that I would return someday full of tales and then I was out the door.

As I walked across the gravel yard between buildings, I noticed that several of the guests were milling about at the edge of the adjacent farmyard, pointing toward the bulge in the ground where the Big Bertha shell lay under a tarp. Delaying his plowing until the guests had all departed, Thijs was careful to hold everyone back from the site while at the same time describing the destructive power of the shell when its equals struck Old Ypres during the War. "It took crews consisting of hundreds of German soldiers to set up the Big Bertha howitzer in the Houthulst Forest, north of here. Once zeroed in, each of these shells was capable of bringing down entire rows of homes in Ypres, which they did. Ypres was nearly entirely destroyed by this weapon alone. How one of these shells landed here and why it did not explode is a question of fate, but I am inclined to think that its power is no less now than when it was launched. I will be far happier when the Bomb Disposal Battalion has taken this shell into their daily inventory and have disposed of it in a routine fashion."

Heads nodded all around.

Like a trusty horse, Max awaited me in the barn. I secured my loaded saddlebags in place and started off, feeling the usual initial pains in my legs and my bum as the unique interface with the bicycle was reestablished. As I rode past the guests near the farmyard, all of them waved to me and smiled. Within a few feet of the entrance to Lark Farm, I stopped to adjust my jacket zipper. My feet were on the ground on either side of Max Mobilier and for what reason I do not know, I looked back at Lark Farm's composite of buildings with a deeper interest. The buildings' colors and shapes were so harmonic and peaceful that it was ironic that they should be situated here, in Flanders, a site of such conflict.

The air was almost still as I cycled my way under a blue sky through diverse farms *en route* to Passchendaele. Finding my way to Bornstraat, I followed it to the southern end of the town, where I turned left onto the small rising lane known as Canadalaan. Just after making the turn to the north on Canadalaan, I stopped by the side of the road to tighten my handlebar. While parked there, certainly atop a point at which a German machine gun nest once lurked, I heard nothing but the mild wind blowing past me. That is, until I heard a faint splash perhaps fifty meters to the east, where a pond no larger than a shell crater lay near an empty drainage ditch. In the center of the pond, a male Little Grebe in the last of its winter coat was diving for its breakfast, shaking watery projectiles in all directions each time it emerged from the depths.

At the top of the hill, the blockish white granite monument to the triumphant Canadian forces graced the center of a small green park square. If viewed from the air, the borders surrounding the monument fulfill the shape of a keyhole, apt considering the tiny aperture of opportunity the Canadians exploited on that rude November 7 when they overwhelmed appropriately named Crest Farm and took the town and somewhat more. I held my cap in my hand as I walked around the site. Looking to the southwest, it was striking to see how gentle was the flow of land to the valley of farmlands with its dots of red brick homes and outbuildings. This was a ridge only in name. Looking to the northeast, Canadalaan extended as a tree-lined village street, leading into the center of Passchendaele and to its church spire. From this vantage point, a stand of maples prevented a southerly glance at massive Tyne Cot Cemetery, but I felt its gravity.

If you were to drop a line between the northeast and southwest corners of the monument and extended it fifteen meters onto the adjacent grass, you would find me, looking now to the southwest, toward Ypres, from which direction the Canadian attack had come. I knew from my reading that despite their careful approaches, the cost of taking Passchendaele was high - nearly 16,000 Commonwealth casualties were inflicted, including over 4,000 dead, all within a half-mile of where I stood. Moreover, the taking of Passchendaele has been seen by many to have been strategically useless, making the event all the sadder.

These were my thoughts as I glided slowly downhill, southwest on Canadalaan.
The tragedy of such loss reminded me of the weeks in the past winter when my marriage suddenly fell apart. After what I recalled as happy decades together, Lois had informed me that she would be leaving me for a neighbor of relatively recent vintage. We did spend the requisite few weeks with counselors and the like but she was always resolute and I somehow had no doubt from the outset that she would carry out her wishes. I put on a good show, even helping with the dismantling of the connectedness of most of our physical and financial possessions in order to avoid undue conflict. In the end, at least I still had a home to return to. Certainly, I drank a bit more in those weeks and in the ensuing months - but not that much more.

She was probably correct in her complaint that I had become usual, imperturbable and no longer a source of excitement to her. Awareness of this came as quite a blow to me, as I had always fashioned myself as someone who lived, if anything, too rich a fantasy life for a Brit. Her message, though, was that whether I had such an inside life or not, my flaw was my inability to express it. Therefore, it was to her as if it had never existed at all. We were each old enough to know that personal change is improbable, so we left it all with a simple British peck on the cheek and it was over.

It was after many cold dinners later that I began to consult my colleagues about useful distractions, such as this trip. Consequently, I found myself at that moment at the intersection of Bornstraat and Canadalaan, looking once again at the pond for that energetic Little Grebe. But he had moved on.

Chapter 9. Tyne Cot

In a reverse of the Canadians' advance in 1917, I sped down the Passchendaele's slope toward Tynecotstraat, braked noisily and made an acute left turn. Then I was climbing again toward the entrance to fabled Tyne Cot Cemetery, the largest cemetery in the world that is maintained by the Commonwealth War Graves Commission of England. Tyne Cot sprawls over a ridge of high land that was hotly contested by both sides in the war but which was mainly held and fortified by the Germans. I parked Max next to a building at the far right front corner of the cemetery, a building that juts aggressively into the roadway. I then walked along the front wall of the cemetery to the main gate, which is composed of dark stones fringed with white accent blocks. The gate is a portal, topped with a serially stepped roof. Upon entering the shaded portal, the air is cooler and the scene ahead stops you as you observe. It is as if the portal was designed to adjust you suddenly to the enormity of what you are about to see.

Lying before you, in exquisitely organized fashion, are 11,954 headstones, all chalk white with rounded tops. Each is inscribed with the name and unit of the soldier beneath, except when the soldier was unknown at the time of burial. In those cases, the stones all read the same: "A Soldier of the Great War. Known Unto God." Of the 11,954 headstones, a stunning 8,367 are so inscribed. As I walked into the cemetery, I saw that it had been designed around German pillboxes that had defended this hill with enfilading fire. Two are near the entrance, nearly equidistant from the portal. Sword-like columnar trees surround them, each 20 meters high. Another, positioned all but underground, serves as the base of the prominent and beautiful Cross of Sacrifice that dominates the cemetery. A plaque at its base reads: "This was the Tyne Cot blockhouse captured by the 3rd Australian Division 4 October 1917." The ANZAC forces, attacking from the right flank of the Canadians, had suffered mightily in the attack on Tyne Cot, just as they had in their previous battles. Two additional pillboxes are located beneath domed pavilions on the northeast and southeast corners of the cemetery. These are also largely below ground and are fittingly presently used as gardening sheds by the caretakers of the cemetery.

When I walked behind the Cross of Sacrifice, I noticed that a special set of gravestones - 343 of them, according to my guidebook - were placed in wild disarray, completely in contrast to those in the remainder of the cemetery. A young man in a caretaker's coverall saw me, as I stood absorbed by the scene. He came and stationed himself next to me. He was an odd-looking man, short of stature and very thin, with waxy, alabaster skin, a thin mustache and short, wavy brown hair. He kept his hands in his coveralls when he spoke with a clear but very soft voice. His accent identified him as from Australia or New Zealand, I couldn't quite tell.

"These are the graves of the men who actually died on this hill," he said. "All of the other graves were relocated from temporary cemeteries around Flanders after the war. When the Australians initially captured the field, they turned the main pillbox, under the cross, into a field hospital. As the badly injured men within died, they buried them hastily outside the pillbox, since the area was still under heavy bombardment. There is no rhyme or reason to the orientation of these stones but Sir Herbert Baker, who designed Tyne Cot, wanted to honor those who died here by leaving their graves intact. Those of us who maintain the cemetery take special care of that set of graves, as you can see by the poppies that are planted around the headstones."

He walked with me as I surveyed that unique part of the cemetery and then he asked me to walk with him to the back wall of the cemetery. What looked from a distance like plain white stone was actually a massive inscription of names of soldiers and their units. Extending over two hundred meters, the *Memorial to the Missing* bears the names of nearly 35,000 Commonwealth soldiers who lost their lives in battle and were never found. "These are just the names of the men who died in Flanders after August 15, 1917," he said. The names of the others are inscribed on the Menin Gate in Ypres. After designing the Menin Gate memorial, they realized that it couldn't hold all of the names of the dead, so the *Memorial to the Missing* was built to handle the overflow."

He walked up to one name and put a thin, bony finger on an inscription that read "Liggett O. Storer, Private, 3d Australian Division" and said "This is also my name." The gentle way that he said this had an immediate effect on me and I struggled to hold back a tear. Maybe this was because he mentioned it in such a matter of fact way, just as so many of these men died doing their duty, in a similar, matter of fact way. Or perhaps it was because of the enormity of what I was seeing before me - a sea of death, nearly all of them youths from all over the world - and yet representing not 1% of the forces lost in the war as a whole. And almost all of them, unknown.

When I had composed myself and turned to thank him for the brief tour, he had vanished.

Though the sun was up and the morning was warming, I felt a very slight and brief sheaf of cool air slipping by as I once again turned to face the wall. There, just below Liggett O. Storer's name was the name "Warren A. Storer, Private, 3d Australian Division." Brothers? I wondered, as I contemplated such a tragedy. I turned and walked past the massive, blockish white granite War Stone and then into the area of irregular graves. Near the center of the randomly aligned stones was one that red poppies surrounded almost completely - in marked contrast to the lighter plantings seen around those nearby. Its markings, slightly fainter than those on the wall read "Lawrence A. Storer, Captain, 3d Australian Division. October 5, 1917, Age 32."

Intrigued by the coincidence of names, I activated the browser on my smart phone and searched for their names on the Commonwealth War Graves Commission site. Indeed, they were all brothers, hailing from Polson's Point, Australia, a coastal farming community in the Queensland region. Liggett and Warren had volunteered to join the force together in February 1916 in response to the general call for more troops after the extensive losses of men in the Gallipoli Campaign. Their older brother, Lawrence, had been at Gallipoli and had received a battlefield promotion to Captain. At the time of their enlistment, he was in France, near Armentiere.

After brief infantry training in Australia, Liggett and Warren embarked for the UK together in June 1916. There, they received artillery training at Larkhill, two kilometers from Stonehenge in the Salisbury Plain. They arrived in France in November 1916, when they were reunited with Lawrence, now their commander. They all fought together in the Battles of Messines and Broodseinde Ridge. They became inseparable, until that fateful October morning when Liggett and Warren, according to field hospital notes that were transcribed as Lawrence lay dying, were struck directly by an enemy artillery shell. Lawrence, seeing them beside him no more and injured himself, found cover in the shell hole where they had just been standing. He was retrieved that evening, taken to the pillbox-field hospital, where he recounted what he had seen before expiring from blood loss.

Soon thereafter, a telegraph reached Polson's Point, that distant corner of Australia and of the world, bearing the news to a middle aged couple that their three wonderful sons would not be returning to them. I imagined the couple walking the short distance from their sugar cane farm to the shore of the Coral Sea, looking across the Great Sandy Strait to Fraser Island as whale pods frolicked between the land masses, full of life. Why I thought this, I do not know. I saw them standing there, contemplating their loss, as three humpback whales broke the surface not far from shore. In a slow, twisting cetacean motion, they threw their magnificent bodies high into the air, carrying tons of water skyward as they did. After hanging motionless at their apogees for the briefest of moments, they each shook projectiles of water all around them as they plummeted, ever faster and inevitably, back into the sea. The last of the three to reenter waved its flukes in a sad farewell that seemed to occupy an unusual amount of time. The circular wave emanating outward from where they reentered then grew ever wider and ever more subtle until, in moments, it was not perceptible at all.

As a small group of happy schoolchildren entered the cemetery portal with their teacher, I took one last full look around Tyne Cot. Until now, I had been its only visitor. With this new backdrop of bright voices, the depth of my feelings began to lighten and I knew that it was time to leave. First, though, I wanted to see one of the pillboxes that lay beneath each of the domed, arched pavilions at either end of the *Memorial to the Missing*. I walked slowly over to the one at the southeast corner of the wall and looked at the top of the dome. Through the blinding morning sunlight, I could see the statuette atop, a winged female figure, her head bowed over a wreath. Beneath the floor of the domed pavilion, the remnant of the old pillbox could be seen, along with a short path that led to its side. At the base of a short set of steps leading downward was a brown wooden door. The door was ajar, so I stepped down and looked inside. The room was dark except for the light that came in from the doorway and the old pillbox gunnery slits. Gardening tools of all types were arranged carefully on the walls and there was a small table with chairs in the middle of the room. A burly, middle-aged man in caretaker's coveralls was sitting at the table, repairing a hoe.

"May I help you?" he asked.

A bit at a loss for words, I replied, "No, I was just curious about this structure."

"Old pillbox from the Great War," he said. "The Germans sat right here as they mowed down our boys. Ironic, isn't it, that it now houses all of the tools we use to keep this cemetery looking sharp for those same boys?"

I nodded. I was about to leave when I asked him "You must work with Liggett Storer then, correct?" He gave me an odd look and then slowly said, "There's no Liggett that works here. Why do you ask?" I replied, "I must be confusing the name. I'm sorry to have disturbed you." We made our leave, and I stepped back outside into the warming air and began a stroll down the southern inside wall of the cemetery. The activity in the homes nearby was increasing, and more school buses on tours were disgorging their children. I turned to the right along the entrance wall, found the entry portal, stopped for a moment to sign the register and once again stepped out onto Tynecotstraat. I retrieved Max, checked to see that my saddlebags were in order, pedaled around the corner to Vijwegestraat and rode the short southward spur to Schipstraat, where I turned right. I then rode on, with the sun on my back and a burgeoning Flanders wind in my face, a perplexed heart lying in between.

Chapter 10. Vancouver Corner

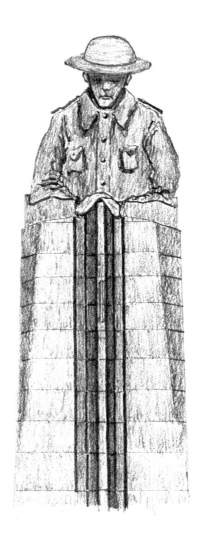

I came to this trip unprepared for the sights that I would see or the feelings that I would experience.

Just days before, in London, I was conversing over tea with my old friend Emil Lazarus, our Chief of Staff. Emil is one of those ever-trusted colleagues with whom you can speak of anything, knowing that your words, though collected and thought through by him, pass via a one-way glass, never to be reflected. He asked about my upcoming small vacation, and I explained that I had purchased a bicycle and was planning to tour West Flanders for a little break. He nodded and then gently said something that surprised me: "It will change your life."

When I asked him why, a tear came to his eye, and he explained that he had made the same trip some years before to visit sites that his grandfather had often spoken about before he died. His grandfather, a long-standing Magistrate in Norfolk, had lived to the age of eighty-five, despite losing his right leg and left arm in a close-fought assault on the Messines Ridge after the sappers had detonated the landscape there in 1917.

As I listened carefully to Emil, I learned the following. His grandfather had been a corporal in the British Second Army under the command of General Herbert Plumer, providing logistical support for the tunnel diggers who placed twenty-two ammonal-containing mines under the Messines Ridge during a year of digging. The 'clay-kickers,' as they were known for their seated tunneling technique, needed an immense amount of support from ground troops who assisted with the translocation of earth that had to be hidden from enemy observers on the high ground. The work started on January 1, 1916. During that year, while the twenty-two main shafts were being dug through the blue clay soil stratum at approximately thirty meters below the German front lines, multiple secondary diversion shafts were dug in shallower soil to confuse German counter miners. Despite these efforts, the Germans found one of the ammonal-containing mines and defused it, also destroying the shaft.

Ammonal is an industrial explosive containing variable amounts of an oxidizer, ammonium nitrate, an explosive, trinitrotoluene (TNT) and a power enhancer, aluminum powder. Ammonal absorbs water readily, so the troops had to move it about in sealed metal containers or rubber bags, adding considerably to the difficulty of its storage and placement in the shafts. Tons of ammonal (sometimes as many as twenty) were placed in the main shafts to await detonation. On June 7, 1917, seven hundred Commonwealth guns maintained an extensive artillery barrage on Gruppe Wijtshate of the German Fourth Army, situated on the Messines Ridge. When the barrage ended, as was the usual practice, the German troops retook their forward positions in expectation of an Infantry attack.

Soon thereafter, they were in the process of being relieved by fresh troops - and therefore temporarily at double strength - when their world exploded.

Within one minute, nineteen of the twenty one remaining mines were detonated, creating a blast that could be heard as far away as London and Dublin, lifting the top of the ridge away and destroying the village of Messines. The Germans instantly sustained 10,000 fatalities and 25,000 overall casualties occurred in the day's fighting that ensued. Two mines were not detonated, as they were not located directly beneath the German-occupied front. One of these remaining mines would accidentally detonate in a 1955 lightning storm, killing a cow. The other has never detonated and presently sits beneath a bucolic farmhouse and barn near Messines.

A small farm in Belgium waits for the next shoe to drop.

Immediately after the blasts, Commonwealth artillery began a combination of fixed and creeping shrapnel barrages as its forces rapidly advanced toward their objectives in what ultimately became a complete rout of the Germans. "My grandfather was one of the British boys attacking that hill," Emil said softly. "He was part of the first unit to approach the site that is now known as the Spanbroekmolen crater, below which the largest concentration of ammonal had been cached."

He continued: "Unfortunately for him, as he advanced, he became enmeshed in a Medusa head of falling barbed wire that had been thrown into the sky by the initial blast. An errant British artilleryman soon thereafter placed a large shrapnel charge within ten meters of his exposed position. Two whirling shards of metal, which once had been corn scythes in Deopham Green, whistled without restraint through the multiple layers of the barbed wire that enveloped my grandfather before cleanly severing first his right thigh and then his left arm from his torso. Only rapid application of tourniquets by his mates saved his life. He lay trapped in wire beneath the newly formed ten-meter-high lip of the Spanbroekmolen crater until nightfall, when a team bearing fence cutters was able to release him from his terrible nest. They carried his leg beside him on the stretcher as he held his left arm with his right, looking often and with anguish at his left hand and forearm, by then in rigor mortis."

Emil continued. "Over the years, I had always wanted to see that site as both a tribute to him and to better understand his bravery. Soon after he died, I made a pilgrimage, doing it just as you will do, by bicycle. After a long day of cycling from Zeebrugge, I arrived at the edge of the Spanbroekmolen crater. I was alone, and the wind tousled my hair as I first toured the adjacent Lone Tree Cemetery, where his arm and leg lie buried, unmarked, with the body parts of other unfortunates. I then stood on the earthen lip at the edge of the crater itself, near, I am sure, to where my grandfather was so terribly injured. The crater itself is about eighty meters in diameter and is said to be twelve meters deep. Of course, you cannot see the bottom today because the crater is filled with water. Ironically, the pond is now called the *'Peace Pool.'* Trees surround the crater, and lily pads adorn the surface. Turtles sit atop the lily pads, small fish create brief circles on the water where they suck in midges and mayflies and there is abundant bird life about."

Emil paused before continuing. "As I stood there alone, something fundamental changed within me. I was finally able to fathom just how much humanity sacrificed in that terrible war. Before then, it was all too abstract for me. Then, as if to reinforce the fusion of man's nature with that of broader nature itself, I watched a multicolored wood duck leading two ducklings across the *Peace Pool*. Painting one large and two tiny wakes onto the surface of the water, they made good progress together. Suddenly, from the periphery of my vision, I saw the water rise in a fast-moving mound that was about a meter in length, just behind the trailing duckling. In an instant, the duckling was gone and a lithe green cylinder of fins and muscle propelled itself into the deep. The mother duck became frantic, shielding her other duckling from the pike with a wing whose feathers were trembling in instinctive fear and rage. Fortunately, the two were able to reach the lip of the crater and dry land before I departed. Shaken. Nigel, I promise, you will be a changed man when you return."

As I pedaled past the junction of Roeselarestraat where the road becomes Keerzelaarstraat, I made a mental note to send Emil a periodic email as my trip went on. If anyone would understand the things I was seeing, he would.

Lost in reflection on Emil's words, I nearly plummeted Max and myself into a deep drainage ditch when a large brown and grey Osprey carrying a dazed but wriggling whitefish in its talons crossed the road at a low level just two meters in front of me. They were so close that I could smell both the bird and the fish as they flew past. In tracing its trajectory back to where it originated, I saw that it had emerged from a large farm pond on my right. The Osprey shed water droplets from its feathers as it gained altitude and headed to the west.

It soon became clear that its destination was an old windmill that stood out from the plain adjacent to two old red-roofed barns, half a kilometer ahead. As that was my next destination, I watched with interest as the Osprey circled the tower of the windmill and settled into a large nest it had built on the ledge of one of its uppermost windows. I could see as I approached that two young Ospreys were also in the nest, each vying for the now still fish in their mother's talons.

The windmill was ancient and perhaps twenty meters tall. It was grey-brown, with a peaked roof and huge blades, the lowermost of which cleared the ground by a mere meter. The blades had white tapered leading edges and red support beams, trailed by an open latticed grid work. Man-sized beams at its base that rested in a thatched array on four stone pillars supported the entire structure. The blades were still. Located at the junction of Keerzelaarstraat and Waterstraat, its tower provided by far the best view of the countryside from any location on the local Flanders plain. This is why the Germans used it as an artillery observation tower, from which many a barrage was directed. That it withstood the shelling that it received at the hands of Canadian and British artillerymen is a wonder. It now stands dark and looming, enlivened only by raptors. Where once binoculars peered about, a sharper vision now prevails.

I took some photographs of the windmill, sent one to Emil with a short note and consulted my watch. Eleven am. I was due to meet Helen and James at *The Arrow* in Poelcapelle in an hour. It would take me about twenty minutes to ride northeast to the restaurant, even with the wind at my back. So I mounted Max and proceeded swiftly along Onze-Lieve-Vrouwstraat to the junction with a minor highway known as Zonnebekestraat. After riding for only five hundred meters, I arrived at the intersection with the bustling N313 highway, otherwise known as Brugseweg.

I had arrived at 'Vancouver Corner,' so named during the war by Canadian forces that fought nearby.

I parked Max under some cedar trees that had been pruned to look like shells and walked toward the imposing monument there that is known as "the Brooding Soldier." At the summit of an eleven-meter tall plinth of solid white granite rises the sculpture of a soldier, from mid torso up, his head bowed in reverence, his hands holding a rifle. On the front of the column the word "CANADA" is inscribed. On its southern side is a plaque that reads:

THIS - COLUMN - MARKS - THE BATTLEFIELD - WHERE - 18,000 CANADIANS - ON - THE - BRITISH LEFT - WITHSTOOD - THE - FIRST GERMAN - GAS - ATTACKS - THE - 22-24 APRIL 1915 - 2,000 - FELL AND - LIE - BURIED - NEARBY

The monument, facing Canada, is striking in its simplicity. From my guidebook, I learned that the trees and other foliage around the monument came from many sites in Canada. A shrine to the bravery of the Canadian soldier, it was actually designed by a native Briton, Frederick Chapman Clemesha, who emigrated to Regina, Saskatchewan after working for years on tea plantations in Ceylon and then on ranches in Argentina and western Canada. Later to become a noted architect in both Regina and California, he was married on the day that Germany declared war on neutral Belgium. In 1915, despite his Quaker religion, he enlisted in the Canadian forces and served with them for the duration of the war. He sustained a facial injury during his tour of duty, and, like so many other Canadians, he fought at Passchendaele in the Third Battle of Ypres.

Clemesha witnessed great tragedy during his wartime years but none so gruesome as that which he commemorated with his monument. On the 22nd of April 1915, the Second Canadian Division, recently brought into the field as a replacement force, was positioned between French Colonial forces from Algeria and Martinique on its left and British forces on its right flank. The Germans were positioned in entrenchments to the northeast. That night, a very unusual wind arose from the northeast, directly opposite the prevailing Flanders wind direction, from the southwest. Unbeknownst to the Allied forces, the

Germans had more or less evenly distributed along their forward trenches 5,730 cylinders containing one hundred sixty eight tons of chlorine gas. At their officers' signals, German troops opened the valves on their tanks and heavier-than-air chlorine gas slowly drifted toward the Allied trenches.

The French forces were the first to feel its effects.

Stunned by the visible cloud coming toward them and feeling the initial effects of respiratory irritation, they retreated en masse, leaving a seven-kilometer hole in the Allied line. The Canadians were called up in groups along with the British to plug this gap. Thousands of these soldiers died either then or soon thereafter of the asphyxiation that accompanies chlorine gas exposure. The Germans did not exploit the gap for fear of the remaining gas, and the Canadians and British held the field after multiple significant counterattacks. These included the vital Battle of Kitcheners Wood, a bayonet attack through wire that played back and forth over previous French force cooking stations. There would be several other German gas attacks in the sector before the Allies responded in kind, primarily with mustard gas whose effects were even more insidious than chlorine gas.

Clemesha's design was awarded second place in a competition sponsored by the Canadian Battlefield Monument Commission in 1920. The winning design sits atop Vimy Ridge in France, but in contrast, that monument is a far more imposing and less subtle creation than Clemesha's. By the time the monument was dedicated in 1923, Clemesha had already moved to California to pursue his architecture career. He is said to have died there in 1958, having left his best-known work to the world nearly a lifetime before and an ocean away.

As I walked around the circular fieldstone base of the monument, I noticed that it was crenellated in four spots, each bearing an inlay where an arrow of stone pointed to towns on the horizon. I walked Max around to the one that read "Poelcapelle," swung my leg over the seat and began to pedal northeast up Brugseweg. Oddly, I noticed some difficulty in riding. Then I realized that the wind had shifted and was now coming directly from the northeast. The going had become difficult, even though the terrain remained flat.

By the time I reached *The Arrow* in Poelcapelle, my breathing was ragged. I took my pulse. One twenty. I sat outside the restaurant for a few minutes imagining what a chlorine-induced progressive asphyxia might be like. As I recovered my breath, I watched tall cedar trees swaying nearby, half bent over in the wind. The clouds, which that morning had been gently plowing through the sky toward the northeast, were now coming back at high speed. Moreover, they now appeared to be much lower to the ground, dense, dark and sinister.

I inserted Max into the bike rack by the side door and entered *The Arrow*. There were Helen and James in the rear, each with a Bloody Mary in hand. They waved energetically, beckoning me over.

Chapter 11. The Arrow

Helen and James were full of smiles when I arrived, their cheeks noticeably ruddier than when I had left them that morning. "Welcome to *The Arrow*," they said in unison, as James withdrew a menu that he had been holding upright as a blocking screen, revealing a celery and pepper-laden Bloody Mary that was meant for me. As I slid into the bench next to James, Helen advanced the drink to me, saying, "You must have had a hard ride in that wind. We noticed its force even in the car, while driving here from Ypres. I am sure that something bloody will fortify you."

"There's nothing quite like having the perfect beverage at the ready after a strenuous endeavor," I concurred, raising my glass in a toast to their warm hospitality. We all drank deeply of our crimson liquids. "What did you see?" they asked. I recounted my trip to Tyne Cot, and especially my odd encounter with Liggett O. Storer, described the frightening, airy brush-by of the Osprey and the subsequent visit to the observation windmill, finally related my feelings as I stood before the Brooding Soldier. They indicated that they had just come from that sculpture themselves, and they'd been moved, as well. But that the bulk of their morning had been spent at Essex Farm, the nearby Yorkshire Trench and at the *In Flanders Fields* museum in Ypres.

They were touched, they said, to stand at Essex Farm, near the site where the poem "In Flanders Fields" was written. "James actually cried," Helen said, (as he blushed). They also were surprised by the depth and structure of the actual trenches, exposed by the Diggers, a local preservationist group that had uncovered the Yorkshire Trench, close by.

However, it was the museum in Ypres that filled them with the greatest awe. "You must see it today, Nigel," James urged. "It is filled with the war's cause and effect in powerful detail. The museum genuinely reflects what those who endured the war must have seen and felt, including the sounds of the war. These are all around you in the museum. Even aircraft can be heard, buzzing low, strafing troops and dropping bombs."

At that, James turned to me and asked, "Speaking of bombs, do you know why they call this restaurant *'The Arrow'*?"

"I haven't a clue...why?"

"Last evening, after a bottle or two of wine, we asked the owner about it. At first, he was reluctant to say. He said it was a local secret. So we did the Canadian thing and bought him a drink or two and sat him down with us and eventually asked him again. By then, he was ready to tell us.

Even third hand, it was a fascinating story. In the Great War, aircraft were used heavily for reconnaissance and also for gunnery attacks on the enemy. The Germans, who in peaceful moments used to enjoy dining outside in the old restaurant that stood here then, called The Poel, occupied this field. They dined while seated on what is now the patio of *The Arrow*. When the Allies began to fly larger and stronger aircraft over the area, the Germans began to assign heavier and heavier guns to air defense and wound up hitting many of these aircraft and bringing them down.

One of these guns was adjacent to the restaurant itself. When Allied pilots survived after crashing in the region, one German officer, an Adjutant Colonel, summarily executed them. His name, oddly enough, was Mannfreund Gott. Mannfreund Gott became well known as a brutal enemy, not only to the Allies but also to the villagers of Poelcapelle. He encouraged his men to take license with the people and the possessions of the village, including its women, and all hated him.

In war, there are spies everywhere. The people of Poelcapelle made sure that the Allied forces knew that Adjutant Colonel Gott was the man responsible for the execution of their pilots - and what his common habits were. The Allies then devised a cruel plan of their own.

Gott enjoyed taking his noontime meal alone at the outdoor table at the Poel, near the anti-aircraft gun. A glutton, he would sit for hours consuming outsized portions of rationed goods. A typical lunch might be a green salad decorated with hard-boiled egg and small pieces of stewed rabbit, thyme-roasted potatoes and braised venison, paired with a carafe or two of claret. Eventually he would fall asleep in his chair. One day, he nodded off a bit earlier than usual. Perhaps someone laced his food, who knows?

It was common at the time for Allied pilots to drop heavy iron arrows from their aircraft onto German trenches, with sometimes gruesome results. On a particular day in July, 1917, a warm and beautiful day, Officer Gott slept at his table when an echelon of eleven Sopwith Camels flew directly toward him very low overhead and rained one hundred and ten iron arrows down upon his table. Their pattern when they struck was promiscuous in their overlap upon and near him. Thirty penetrated Gott himself, twelve his dinner and the remainder created a small fence around him that prevented access to him for at least the few moments that it took for him to die.

What was never explained, because the townspeople found him first and removed it before German troops arrived, was the single highly lacquered and personally signed wooden Belgian hunting arrow that was found deeply embedded in his heart. Its owner and deliverer was never identified by the Germans but was well-known to the villagers, who never divulged the archer's name, an enduring example of the unity of this tiny community. That is why the restaurant is called 'The Arrow.'

Just then, the owners, burly, dark haired Luc van Gustart and his very petite blonde wife, Eline, stopped by our table. They addressed Helen first, saying that they had looked throughout the restaurant for her lost phone, but found no trace of it, despite James ringing it several times. Helen and James accepted the loss as one of travel's little glitches. After an accepting gesture of their hands, we all smiled, reached for the last ounces of our Bloody Marys, lifted them twice, in the Belgian style, and tipped off their contents.

Luc and Eline stepped away for a moment and brought us each a glass of lightly bubbling Prosecco. "An aperitif," he explained, "to prepare you for what we hope will be a lovely meal for you." Pouring a glass for themselves as well, they sat with us and translated the menu, which was in Dutch.

"Voorgerechten," Luc said, "Are the traditional meal starters – you call them 'appetizers.' We are proud to serve all of them but we would recommend that on this cool, windy day we bring you all one large warm starter, a group portion of Eline's special *moules frites,* to warm you up." We agreed and were happily surprised when Eline invited us all to the open kitchen area to watch her prepare them. James, Helen and I grasped our glasses of Prosecco lightly as we strode past animated groups of local diners, speaking happily in Dutch as we approached the overlook area just above the top step to the kitchen.

Eline and Luc took up their stations with evident comfort, Eline at the stove and Luc at the prep table. On the great gas range, Eline already had a stock brewing, to which she added a half-liter of a white *vin de table* Bordeaux and a small bottle of Duvel beer. As the pot began to simmer, her deft hands first chiffonaded a grip of parsley leaves and then one of celery leaves. She then minced a shallot, a clove of garlic, a celery stalk and a carrot - all of which went into the broth, followed by the off white-green rings of a large leek that floated on the surface momentarily before each ring tipped an edge into the surface and was lost from view. Some of the leeks resisted this fate, oscillating on the surface, looking as though they would not succumb to heat and physical force. These, however, ultimately fell the most vertically into the fluid. As the stock assumed a roiling motion, the leeks periodically came to the surface, as did bits of the other vegetables, only to be swallowed back into its depths. The leeks were fascinating to watch. With each reemergence, they shed yet another outer ring until, like trees aging in reverse, they lost all of their maturity and succumbed to the heat and the depths, all rings apart, children again.

Reaching into the utensil drawer, Eline removed three spoons and showed them to us. Their silver contrasted nicely with her black blouse and navy blue apron, creating a fine Fleur de Lys pattern as she held them splayed symmetrically upright by the ends of their handles. "These are the secret to seasoning," she said, with a twinkle of a smile and a glint in her eye. She then dipped one spoon into the broth to capture a sample, let it cool and tasted it with her eyes closed. "Aah, she said - almost but not quite there." She reached for the salt jar and using the thumb and all of the fingers of her right hand, she reached into the salt to an apparently preimagined depth and like a mechanical tree remover, lifted an inverted cone of salt from the jar, sprinkling it vigorously into the pot. To it she also added multiple grindings from what was clearly an ancient pepper grinder.

After stirring the pot briefly, she sampled the broth again using spoon two, eyes once again closed. "Beautiful but needing just that little bit extra," she said, as she grated a bit more pepper and this time grasped only the salt that she could hold between the tips of her thumb, index and middle fingers, adding it to the pot and stirring. Eline then tasted from spoon three, opened her eyes and smiled - "Now it is perfect," she said. Using a large ladle, she transferred perhaps a liter of the broth to another large pot and brought it to a boil. Reaching behind her into the service refrigerator, she used a small measuring bucket to transfer three large portions of well cleaned and tightly closed mussels into the pot and covered it with a tight lid. Luc was busy debearding and cleaning more mussels at the prep table.

Eline now retrieved three large portions of previously julienned, snow white potato pieces from the refrigerator. They had been sitting in water, emitting their own excess starch. Eline rinsed them and shook them in a basket to remove their attached water film, then dried them with a rich, thick terry cloth towel. Then, in batches, she transferred them to an enormous fryer that was decidedly hot, by all appearances from the observation deck. After several minutes of careful watching and waiting, Eline removed their holding basket and tipped the now lightly golden *frites* onto a board covered with paper, where they briefly drained. As they did so, she reached into the cupboard and removed a large enameled metal service pot with handles. Setting the oven to low, she inserted it inside to warm for a short period.

Seeing that our glasses were now empty, Eline took pity upon us, set up three new stems and poured us the remains of the Bordeaux, so we could remain nourished as we watched her finalize the preparation. Wasting no time, she scooped up the frites and added them once again to the fryer. Seemingly in moments, she retrieved them, now deeply golden, briefly drained them, and arranged them in paper cones set up in conical wire coils. Then she removed the service pot from the oven, took off the lid from the pot containing the mussels, poured the contents - wide open mussels, including the steaming broth - into the service pot and then bade us retreat to our places as she and Luc served us the steaming mussels and *frites*. As Eline delivered a mussel shell discard bowl to the table, she also set a dining plate before each of us as well as two small, empty bowls.

Luc then stood by the table with a mysterious look on his face.

We were all ready to devour this beautiful feast when he said to us: "You know, in Flanders, this is the moment of truth," then smiled as he held his hands behind his back. We looked at one another, perplexed, as he reached forward with both hands, one holding an elaborate serving tureen containing a spoon and mayonnaise, the other a bottle of Heinz 57 ketchup. "Which would you prefer to garnish your *frites*?" he said, almost in a mocking tone. A brief silence ensued. James said, "When in Rome..." Luc smiled as he then ladled out three large dabs of mayonnaise. He then stepped away as we alternated eating mussels and *frites* until finally, there were just a few withered leeks in the broth and a few crumbs in the paper cones.

Luc soon returned to the table with a dusty bottle of *Chateau Neuf de Pape*, uncorked it, poured four glasses and sat down with us to confer regarding the *Hoofdgerechten*, the main courses. Of course, he brought with him a platter containing Passendale cheese. We proceeded to enjoy these delectables as we sipped the wine and watched Luc contemplating the menu's suggestions. Suddenly, he looked up, closed the menu and said, "How about if you let me surprise you?" We nodded. Luc strode over to the kitchen where we could hear him conferring with Eline for a few moments. They went into action together.

Helen, James and I, meanwhile, were in a fine state of cheer after so many libations. We began to speak of our plans for the remainder of the day. James spoke first. "Helen and I plan to visit Tyne Cot, then head south to the Passchendaele Museum in Zonnebeke, after which we hope to have time to visit Hill 60 and its little museum, too. Afterwards, we need to get settled at the Menin Gate in Ypres, since the organizers have asked us to appear by 7:30. We will lay our wreath at the Gate as part of the 8:00 pm ceremony. You may not believe this but we plan to dine again tonight, at the *Ramparts Bistro* near our new hotel. What are your plans?"

I took a largish swallow of the wine, ensuring that a bit of bread and cheese would reach my stomach at terminal velocity before I responded. "My plan is nowhere near as ambitious. I intend to ride, now with the wind, to the Ijser Canal and follow it to Essex Farm. I will only be able to spend a short time there, as I will need to get to Ypres long enough before museum closing time to enjoy the *In Flanders Fields* museum, too. I hope to see you two laying your wreath at the Menin Gate. My plan is to stay at the hotel that is attached to the *Ramparts Bistro*, where I also hope to dine, so we may revisit this festival there." We clinked glasses once again.

Then James brought up an odd experience that he had had at Lark Farm, while checking out. He said, "When we went into the business office near the kitchen to pay our bill, Thijs was at the desk, doing some paperwork. The maid, Marijke, was behind him, in the kitchen, wiping pots with a towel. Helen and I exclaimed to him that we thought Lark Farm was a delightful place and that we particularly enjoyed Paula's enthusiastic hospitality. We were fairly gushing when Thijs said in his slow English "It's a shame, but Paula wants to be leaving here." He nearly wept as he recounted that he felt that he had more to do on this land, but she wanted to get out now and see the world and tell it about Flanders. "I can accept what she wants to do," Thijs said, "but it will be hard for me and the children to run this place without her and to also maintain the farm. And we haven't settled the finance part of our separation."

James said, "We were just struck by how utterly forthright he was and by Paula's surprising decision. Once in the car, we looked at each other, stunned, before driving off. One more thing. As Thijs was speaking, I looked into the kitchen at Marijke, who had just partially turned away. I could swear that she had a sly smile on her face. I must say that I left Lark Farm more unsettled than when I had entered."

At that moment Luc and Eline returned with our entrees. Each was covered with a silver dome, which enhanced our anticipation. They opened their serving racks and set down the trays. Helen was served first. Eline set her plate before her and with a quick extension of her delicate wrist, removed the cover, releasing a brief, obscuring cloud of steam. In French, Eline said "*Marcassin des Flandres avec chouc de Bruxelles a la Flamande,*" and then followed in English "Pork loin braised in red wine with Flemish style Brussels sprouts." Helen's delight was evident. She smiled and thanked Eline, took a sip of her wine and watched as Luc set to work on the entrees.

James's dish was opened next. "Fried pheasant, chicory with slenders of orange and chocolate on porcini mushrooms in an herbed broth accompanied by endives au gratin." James was astonished at the creative array situated around the gleaming bird and by the deep aroma of Swiss cheese issuing from the ham-enveloped endives. He put his large, contented hands on his belly and said, "It looks wonderful. Now, let's see what you have for our friend Nigel."

Eline moved to the larger serving tray that Luc had carried out. The last cover was taller and narrower than the others. She held her small hand on the peak of the dome for a moment, turned to me and said "Luc and I saw you ride in on a bicycle with saddlebags, so we assumed that you might still have a bit of hard riding to do today. We wanted to make you a special dish that will keep you warm and will also give you strength as you ride." With that she placed the dish before me and removed the cover. When the steam cleared, I saw a complex stew containing beans, potatoes, carrots and several types of fish in chunks. One type was darker, which I assumed might be eel. All of its pieces were swimming in a rich, yellow-white broth. Its aroma enveloped me. It was just the meal I needed.

"Gentse waterzooi," Eline said. It is a simple dish and has been a real staple of our local cuisine for many lifetimes." She was pleased at my positive reaction. She then reached into her apron and placed two types of bread on the table. She first replenished the type of baguettes we had had before. She also placed a cutting board out, atop which she placed a round, crusty loaf with a gash in its top. "Belgian *verviers* bread - a little bit of sweetness to go with your meals." Then she bowed and departed.

We all immediately began exploring our dishes. Helen found her pork loin to be especially tender and the reduction coated each slice in a fine, flavorful glaze. The nutmeg in her Brussels sprouts set off the entire complex of tastes in the pork, accentuated as they were by the micro-fracturing texture of the sprouts. James, sitting next to her, attacked his pheasant with anatomical gusto. Clearly a carver, he first disarticulated all of its joints with oddly accurate vertical insertions of his small knife into the joint capsules, made small twists and the bird immediately devolved into multiple pieces.

James let these sit on the moist mushrooms as he attended to the breast meat. He laid the torso of the bird on its back, steadied it with a fork, and then found the parasternal seam between the ribs and the origins of the flight muscles. On each side, he employed a light reversed 'C' motion, mapping his stroke to the curve of the vertebrae while separating the breast meat from each side in one skilled back and forth exercise. Once he had separated the breast meat, he set both ovoid breasts flat on the mushrooms and sliced each at attractive angles so as to expose the largest possible face of each slice to the mushroom broth. He then sliced a baguette, buttered it and ate each piece of the bird with some mushrooms and a small bite of the bread. Wine lubricating each step, naturally. He then set upon his endives, riven as they were with liberal doses of ham and cheese, as I enjoyed my *Waterzooi*.

The bowl before me was deeper than I had originally perceived it to be. Maybe this was because the hand painted scene on the glazed inner rim was of Flanders farmlands, which my instincts inclined toward considering always to being flat. The effect of the depth was to maintain the heat of the dish and also, of course, to overwhelm me with nourishment. As is my habit when I have a curry in London, I began by sipping the broth, sometimes while dunking a corner of baguette and chewing on that, too.

However, as I began to appreciate that the broth contained both egg yolks and cream, I realized that the broth could be best enjoyed as a full accompaniment to the generous pieces of vegetables and fish, so I alternated spearing, dipping and eating them with additional small pieces of the baguette. The resulting experience was a bit like enjoying a multi-component fondue that was very satisfying and filling. As I reached the deepest part of the bowl, I could see that its hand painted design had changed to depict the fertile roots of plants, the generous water table and a series of pristine irrigation canals, all shown in sagittal section, as if one were underground, looking through transparent soil. The anatomy of a region. As I sipped the last bit of creamy broth from the bowl, I saw that the design of the bowl, solidly visible once the soup was spent, had been dated.

'1910,' it read.

As each of us completed our dishes, we began to look at one another once more, this time with even fuller and happier faces. We clinked our glasses and sipped again as Helen reached for the second loaf of bread and sliced it for us. As she did, we could hear the faint sound of a blade pushing through crushed glass. Interested, we all bent over to look at the bread and saw that it was riddled with small sugar cubes. These gripped the butter we applied and we all enjoyed a bit of sweetness before Luc and Eline returned to collect our plates.

With the table once again clear, save for our remaining wine, James said, "For years, I have wanted to visit this area and pay homage to my grandfather and great uncles. They were all part of the assault on Passchendaele during which only my grandfather survived. Though he was unwounded, he unfortunately witnessed the deaths of his brothers, one of whom received a head wound, was evacuated and died two days later at the Ste. Juliaan dressing station. The other, his younger brother, in an attack ahead of him, was perforated in his upper torso by machine gun fire from a German pillbox, fell into the mud and was quickly absorbed. There was no way to fix his position. He was simply lost to sight, almost immediately. My grandfather wept as he fought his way forward. With bitterness, he took the Canadalaan hill with a small contingent of others at the end of the battle. Throughout the years when we visited him on his farm, he would lament his fate as the only family survivor. I promised him on his deathbed that I would visit the Menin Gate to honor his brothers. I am just sad that it has taken me so long to do so."

Eline returned to the table with our dessert, a pie known as *Tarte au Sucre Brun*. She also brought coffee with sugared cream. We stopped our conversation to once again enjoy the fruits of her kitchen. When we had finished the pie, she brought a plate of molasses *speculoos*, the cookie of Belgium, a beautiful, crisp, sweet brown cookie. In this case, they were all crafted in the shapes of arrows. The arrangement was odd. One cookie was longer and of a lighter shade. We all looked quietly at one another as we realized that the lighter and longer cookie was carefully pointed on its plate in the direction of the patio.

After we paid and effusively thanked Luc and Eline. James took me to their car and showed me the wreath he would soon lay. It was a circle of red poppies, vibrant as a young girl's party dress. Its petals shook in the wind as he restored it to its place in the boot, each poppy's black eyes blazing. He shook my hand with two of his and Helen gave me a great hug as her hair blew asunder across both her face and mine. She smelled of nutmeg, I noticed I promised that I would look for them at the Menin Gate and watch to see them lay their wreath. We agreed to meet at the bistro just afterward.

With that promise, I climbed back aboard my poppy-red Max Mobilier and pedaled to the southwest back down Brugseweg, round of belly and fuzzy of mind, the angry wind at my back, alive with anticipation of the sights to come, happy for the marvelous friends I had just made.

Chapter 12. Essex Farm

As I rode away from *The Arrow*, I thought of my digestive tract, carving carbon atoms one by one from that festive lunch to give me life, much as the fertile fields around me did the same to their quiet contents.

The pedaling came easy, as by now I was accustomed to both cycling's poetic repeats as well as to the undulating landscape of West Flanders. A generous tailwind helped me, so I put my legs and my lungs on autopilot and simply observed the air and land around me as I rode. I was headed generally in the direction of the old Ijser Canal that once separated German from Commonwealth lines in this sector. Though it would take me a bit of time to reach the canal, I could already sense its presence, ahead, for the land ever so slightly tilted toward it.

My ride took me past a farm whose weathervane had lost its eastern and western arms, allowing the wind to reorient north and south at its whim. I also passed a home that had a fine-linked fence around its backyard that held thrashing pigeons and cooing doves. A grade school let its students out as I rode by, some children wearing iron grey uniforms, others wearing tan or blue, all of them tussling without apparent reason in the schoolyard, teachers shouting but not being heard amidst the din.

A Skylark landed on my handlebar and rode with me for a bit, all light brown and homely in spring plumage until at a seemingly special moment, it arose, flew before me and beckoned to itself first a score and then hundreds of identical Skylarks, leading me along my path.

We were heading together to Essex Farm, where we arrived, after crossing the Ijser Canal, as one. From its anglophilic name one would expect the farm to be located in England, rather than in west Flanders.

Essex Farm is the site of the Advanced Dressing Station where John McCrae wrote "In Flanders Fields." You cannot enter either the now restored concrete bunker that served as a protected site to care for the wounded or its nearby cemetery without being moved. If the word 'words' can be twisted to become 'sword,' then the opposite is equally true. Like Lincoln's monumental Gettysburg Address on a battlefield half a century before, McCrae distilled a personal response to war into a verbal expression that has stood the test of time. On the one hand, the poem evokes a deep sympathy for the plight of the soldier, especially as manifest in his loyalty to the cause of his nation and the war. On the other, its power is said to have influenced the length of the war through its use in War Bond campaigns, and it particularly helped power the entry of the United States into the war.

Has any other short poem had such a large effect?

I parked Max against one of the concrete arches of the bunker and stepped within. Except for some sawdust on the floor that is periodically replaced by preservationists to create the feeling of the bunker during the war, what I encountered was a dripping concrete cavern with no light and a depth that was only sufficient for three projecting partitions to segregate the sites where the wounded once lay in the cold. The degree of protection from enemy artillery was scant, as McCrae learned when an incoming shell adjacent to the guns that decorated the top of the bunker dismembered his great friend and student, Lt. Alexis Helmer, scant feet away from the healing zone, below.

By the time of the Great War, McCrae, who came from a family with a military tradition (and who was a lover of artillery, himself), had already fought in the Boer War, had become an accomplished academic physician and had written a book on pathology. "Ironic," I thought. I imagined him in this tiny concrete cave, sewing lacerations, amputating limbs and treating the concussed. I pictured him triaging the incoming wounded with a hard eye, sensing who might live and who might die, knowing that his resources were always limited and that the war was always of a far greater ferocity than his beneficence could ever quench. Like all thoughtful surgeons who have had the art thrust upon them by circumstance, I am sure that he questioned his hands and his will as he got up each day to a new session with the maimed.

How odd it must have been for him to have those few minutes on the carriage of a parked ambulance to pen his immortal words, once he had buried Helmer and recited the Chaplain's verses in his absence. McCrae was a very avid and experienced poet, so his words are likely to have come quick and clean to him. Much like death to Helmer.

There are places in this world that touch one. Essex Farm is such a place. After taking a drink of water from a deep, cool well on a bright summer's day, you can feel your insides shiver. This is the experience of being on the same ground where John McCrae wrote his poem. His words were all that were needed to provide English-speaking people with a full sense of both the tragedy of the Great War and the loyal passions - or unquestioning subservience - of the men who fought it.

As I walked into the cemetery adjacent to the bunker on that lonely canal bank, red poppies grew behind periodic headstones, fighting their way through well-cultivated grasses to make their colorful statements. As I looked across the field of headstones, I once again saw the Skylarks. This time, each had alit upon a gravestone, so there was not one stone standing without its avian guardian or guardians. On one stone in particular, multiple Skylarks sat, which piqued my interest.

Alone in the cemetery, I walked over to the headstone and read its inscription:

5750 Rifleman
V.J. Strudwick
The Rifle Brigade
14th January 1916 Age 15

After an interposed crucifix, the stone also read:

Not gone from memory
Nor from love

After a bit of research on my smart phone, I learned that Valentine Joseph Strudwick was a tall farmhand who had lived on tiny Orchard Rd. in Surrey, England, just off Horsham and near St. Aubyn's Church. Like many young men entering the war, he had enlisted well before the minimum age of 16 years - he was perhaps 14 when he joined. Little is known of his actions during the war or how he was killed, but he is considered by many to be the youngest official Commonwealth fatality of the war. His grave was well visited: the grass in front of his grave had been worn away.

Fifteen is no age to sacrifice your life for your country.

Whether as a consequence of cycling in the fresh air, the vast lunch or my emotional reaction to Essex Farm Cemetery, I suddenly felt very tired. Nearby, a white bench with a sturdy back sat in the shade under a larch tree. The bench faced down Row U of the cemetery, the same row on which Strudwick's stone was situated. When I sat down and closed my eyes, I could hear the Skylarks flitting about and chirping, though soon the volume decreased and my chin began its slow tilt downward. The wind sifted about me in gentle, sedating luffs.

As REM sleep moved in, so did the dreams. Just ahead of me in the cemetery row, I saw a farmer with an old style cap and a woman in a frock dress pacing, heads down in front of the Strudwick gravestone. Their moans would periodically carry over to me as a function of the lightly swirling winds. Soon, they were gone, replaced in the same spot by young men in tan uniforms, playing a game of cards at a small table as they laughed and told tales. Then, one at a time, they vanished, leaving only one bewildered comrade behind. The lone tan clad figure gestured here and there and then to himself, as if to ask 'Why?' I watched him as he walked away toward the street opposite the cemetery, the whizzing of bullets and shells all about him, none reaching him. He looked up and down the street, seeing no one. Then, he turned back into the fusillade and simply stood in the middle of the cemetery, arms raised, untouched and unbloodied, in the midst of a miasma of projectiles.

A falling larch cone that landed on my left shoulder awakened me, rolled with improbable grace down my arm and into my upturned hand. I looked up and saw a squirrel on the branch above me, chittering at his lost prize. I set it on the bench for him, stood up slowly and eased away, back to the bunker and to Max and to the byways and the now-whirling air of Flanders. As I mounted Max and began my ride, I looked back to the cemetery where one by one the Skylarks launched from their stony perches, collected themselves into a swarm over the bunker and headed northeast, into the wind, from whence they came.

Once again, I was alone.

Chapter 13. In Flanders Fields

Beginning my ride toward Ypres, I consulted my map to find the best route to the Grote Markt, where I would see the immense Lakenhalle for the first time and the *In Flanders Fields* museum within. The route was direct, fairly short - and slightly downhill - but when I was halfway there slightly after 3 pm, my front tire blew with an unusually sharp retort. Although it took me half an hour to repair it, I still had sufficient time to reach Ypres and the museum and to at least see its highlights. After a brisk ride on busy streets, I found myself at the entrance to the museum. I locked Max up in a stone alcove around a corner, removed my saddlebags, climbed the stairs to the museum, paid the admission fee, checked my belongings and came upon the first feature of that unusual museum.

Upon entry to the museum, you are given a card bearing the name and picture of a soldier, just as if you were a conscript yourself in the war and were entering the battle. At various sites in the museum, you insert the card into a reader and it tells you the soldier's fate at that time of the war. My card was of a young man from Yorkshire.

His name (and I spell it in capitals for a reason stated below) was DEQQUND KNoRS. He was a bit of an overbearing man, it seems. His uniforms all had to be embroidered in these letters (with caps, as indicated) and he had his fellow soldiers address him only as 'KNoRS.' No one understood this peculiarity of his. While in training in England, he proved to be fearless and was no less so when on the battlefield in Belgium. He was always the first over the top of the trench, the first to reach the wire and the first to hurtle into the enemy trench, truncheon and serrated bayonet in hand. All were astonished when he returned unharmed after each attack. He personally caused more dismay to Berliner *Frauen* than any other member of the Commonwealth soldiery in Belgium. In the end, he was specially targeted by German snipers, who watched carefully for the emergence from shadow of any double Q they might sight. It could be said that DEQQUND was the cause of more nearby officers' deaths than any man on the battlefield. At least, this is the story that was told as I stopped at each station in the museum and entered my ID card.

DEQQUND became mythical amongst his fellow soldiers. Everyone wanted to fight by his side, feeling that he was invincible. And for the years 1914-1917, he was. But one day, DEQQUND found himself near Passchendaele in October 1917 in possession of a letter from his father. In it, he learned that his mother had perished, killed by an onrushing streetcar in York as she hastened across the street, smiling, to greet his physician father who had been away in the country.

Upon reading this, DEQQUND sat quietly in the mud of the trench, rats scurrying by as usual, when he suddenly tore off his epaulets and his name badges. Despite orders to the contrary, DEQQUND walked up and over the fire step, no weapons in hand and strode silently and steadily into No Man's Land in the bright sunlight. All the soldiers in the trench he had left behind had their heads down when they heard the harsh, unremitting burst of the German machine guns that ensued. When the guns went silent, all half-expected him to return, as he always did.

But he did not. DEQQUND, the Invincible, was never found.

The reason was clear and banal - it not only rained that night, but the British and German artillery crews made No Man's Land into their personal depositories while testing new guns and new artillery crews. All that initially remained of DEQQUND were two torn textile Qs at his trench post, which were slowly ground into atoms on the wet A Frames in the forward trench as unseeing fellow soldiers trod upon them while mobilizing for attack.

As I removed my card from the reader, I thought, my, but these curators are morbid. But as I went from exhibit to exhibit, the story of DEQQUND KNoRS no longer seemed so odd to me: rather, instead, his was a singular embodiment of the madness of the entire experience of the Great War.

The museum was one of the finest I had ever seen, brilliantly immersing the visitor into history. The first steps into its linear womb outlined the complex origins of the war, a barbed wire entanglement of alliances and blood thirst among leaders (that were never to soldier themselves) that enabled the ignition of the gasoline of warfare. The death of an Austrian Archduke donning what appeared to be a badminton shuttlecock seemed to be the catalyst for the conflagration but in fact, the stage had been set eighty years before, when England officially and in alliance recognized the newly emerging independence of Belgium. Honor demanded that Britain enter the war once neutral Belgium was violated by the German incursion in its activation of the ill-fated Moltke-Schlieffen Plan, which called for a flanking motion through neutral Belgium to quickly conquer France. The plucky Belgian Army, led by King Albert, in this case thwarted the plan. Outnumbered and outgunned, it stalled the German advance long enough to ensure that trench warfare would be the modality of the battle until its very end.

The museum compels one to understand the time it depicts. Its exhibits draw the viewer into not only the harsh aspects of the fighting but also the home-front issues and the emotions of all who participated. While viewing the exhibits, one gets the sense that the combatants were entirely different than people of today. Nearly all were wire thin, for instance - unlike the crowd that presently shambles from presentation to presentation in its great rooms. They also appear to have had a homogeneous earnestness about them, as though there was no cynicism at all in engaging in such a lethal exercise as this. One can feel the romance of the idea of a grand war, even as one recognizes its horrors.

With some haste, I took in all I could before finally reaching the inevitable museum gift shop. Why I was able to find time for this, I do not know, but I am glad that I did. In a well-decorated corner, there lay huddled a regiment of umbrellas that were printed with giant red poppies. I selected one of the largest and had it carefully wrapped and shipped to my home. After all, there was no rain predicted for the next few days of my stay in Belgium, and there would undoubtedly be plenty in England, upon my return. Besides, I needed a meaningful souvenir.

After a brief perusal of the bookrack in the gift shop, I began to feel the same way that I always do when I have been in a museum for too long. I can only stand so much, and then I can't stand any more. After a quick leaf through of posters of byways of Ypres and of regional battlefield carnage, I stopped by a small stand that held a tiny book, *The Poets of the Great War*. I bought it on a whim, collected my saddlebags from the cloakroom, shuttled my way down the Lakenhalle's wide stone stairs, and strode off to the dark alcove that sheltered Max.

Chapter 14. Menin Gate

It was six pm. The daily ceremony at the Menin Gate would not be held until eight.

Perfect, I thought. Beer time.

I dissected Max from the metastasis of bicycles that had followed him into what I had thought was a secret alcove and plumped him on his tires once or twice to be sure that he was fine.

He was.

I replaced and secured the saddlebags and tested their stability twice, for you don't want these rotating into your spokes when at speed, as I have learned the hard way. As I was swinging my leg over the seat, I noticed a very old man, sitting in the rear of the alcove. Or did I? No sooner did I look back than he was gone. From a brick-enclosed *cul de sac*, no less. This gave me a shiver, I must say. I sat for a moment and tried to reconstruct him in my mind. Looking down into the mirrored finish of Max's handlebars, I saw him again. It was my own reflection, shrunken, perhaps projected in time. Odd. My Scotland Yard objectivity returned swiftly then and I was left with the impression that this Max held powers beyond my comprehension, as I stepped to the pedal and thrust us both into the early evening sunlight. I did not have far to go.

The Grote Markt in Ypres is a broad, rectangular square. Guiding Max slowly on the cobblestones, I glided by chocolate shops, dressmakers, carvers of wooden curios, toile weavers, small, inviting hotels, bookstores, coffeehouses and even City Hall. I stopped at one point to look up. You know the posture: one foot on the ground, one on a pedal, torso twisted about. The most interesting things always being behind you. I had learned on a previous trip to continental Europe that what you see at ground level is only the beginning of the visual story of a place. Architects often become their most fanciful when the air gets thinner.

I craned my neck and was not disappointed.

Many of the buildings were structured with step gables. One, the former *Hotel Kasslrij,* had three sets of dormer windows projecting from its roof. I rode over to look more closely at what appeared to be medallions decorating the building. As I inspected them, an elderly

Belgian woman noticed the interest I was taking in them. She set her large grocery bag down walked over to me, and said in perfect English "Those are depictions of the seven deadly sins," as if she had somehow known me all her life. She turned and walked back to her bag, stepping away as if she had just saved the world.

I spotted the patio of the *Ramparts Bistro and Hotel* to my right. A memorable thirst once again overcame me. It must have been an inordinately dry museum, I thought, as I parked Max by a table that faced directly onto the square. When I sat down, it took a bit of time for the server to arrive, so I perched there, looking southward toward the sun and to the roofs of the buildings, opposite. These buildings all looked hundreds of years old, yet I knew that they had all been rebuilt from the ground up after the Great War. In all cases, I noticed large windows everywhere, as though this entire city desired to suck into itself all of the sunlight and its associated joy that it possibly could.

There was also something unusual about the gutter colors of all of the buildings in the square. Each was accentuated by bright paint, and I noticed a repeating pattern on the buildings as my eyes swept from one to another. First, a red gutter, then an orange, and then a yellow. "Could it be?" I thought. Sure enough, these were followed by green, blue, indigo and violet gutters, then the pattern repeated. Ypres, even in its management of the rainfall of life, was pulling from the sun its full spectrum over and over. "And," I thought to myself, "If ever there were a town in the world that deserves to do so, it is this one."

Just then, a pencil-thin woman wearing a black blouse and skirt to which a form fitting starched white apron appeared to be glued, appeared tableside. Her blonde hair was gently done up in a bun. Her fingers were delicate and moved gingerly. Her smile projected a tight little bow. Her nose was small and slightly upturned. Her ears were projecting laterally more than was normal, but this only accentuated her beauty. Alas, it's the plight of the Investigator to notice these little things.

Especially because she looked exactly like my lost wife, Lois.

"What is the best local beer," I asked. She leaned over. I could smell her perfume as she said, "When my friends and I go dancing, I always like to drink Boezinge Ale. It is lighter than most Belgian beers and may be just the thing for a tired cyclist."

I looked up from the menu and said to the harried young man who had been patiently standing by my table ("where did HE come from," I thought) "I'll try a Boezinge." He stepped away with my order.

As I waited for my beer, I retrieved *The Poets of the Great War* from my pocket.

As I flipped through its pages, I noted that the book was devoted to the sixteen English poets who both wore a uniform in WWI and had become famed for their literary art. They were sensitive thinkers who lived in a brutal time, and each in his own way snipered the war with his words. I was too absorbed in reading their history and their works to notice that my Boezinge had arrived (surely a rare omission for me), along with a small basket of brown bread and butter, which I apparently drank and ate mechanically, as my waiter was now back again. With a nod, I was replenished and once again was absorbed in my reading. "Where did that waitress go?" I wondered subconsciously.

Of the sixteen poets who were mentioned in the book, six died in the war. They were Rupert Brooke, Julian Grenfell, Wilfred Owen, Isaac Rosenberg, Charles Sorley and Edward Thomas. Three eighths of Britain's wartime notable poetic force had been fed to the battle. I learned interesting things about these six as I sat there and read.

Rupert Chawner Brooke was 28 and was a sub-lieutenant when he died on St. George's Day, 1915 (April 23, Shakespeare's birthday) en route to the Gallipoli landings. Ironically, he was felled by a mosquito bite on the lip that blossomed into a case of systemic sepsis. From his poem, *"V. The Soldier"* I read:

> *"If I should die, think only this of me:*
> *That there's some corner of a foreign field*
> *That is forever England..."*

Brooke is buried at Tris Boukes Bay on the island of Skyros, one of the Sporades in the mid-Aegean. It was near there that he died aboard the French hospital ship *Duguay-Trouin*. A stately, low-lying tomb made of stone and wrought iron surmounts Brooke's grave. It is positioned on a hilltop and is surrounded by the branches of olive trees. So popular was Brooke that his obituary in *The Times* was written by none other than Winston Churchill.

Almost exactly one month later, Captain Julian Henry Francis Grenfell of the Royal Dragoons died in Boulogne, France from complications of a cranial injury he sustained when a shell splinter struck him thirteen days before, in Ypres. Grenfell was born in London, educated at Eton and Balliol College, Oxford and enlisted in the Army in 1910. Widely known for his machismo and "love of war," Grenfell was indeed quite brave. He was awarded the *Distinguished Service Order* in January 1915 for his part in an especially daring reconnaissance mission. His avowed specialty was the cunning tracking and dispatching of enemy snipers. His most famous poem, *"Into Battle"* was published in *The Times* along with his death notice, a day after he died. One stanza of the poem particularly emphasizes his feelings about war:

> *"And when the burning moment breaks,*
> *And all things else are out of mind,*
> *And only Joy of Battle takes*
> *Him by the throat, and makes him blind."*

Amongst the war poets, the mantle of supreme greatness has oscillated over the years between Rupert Brooke and Wilfred Edward Salter Owen.

Owen was born in Oswestry in the West Midlands. Unable to afford the University of London, he leveraged his regional education to become a teacher. His love for poetry came early but reached its fullest expression under the guidance of fellow Great War poet, Siegfried Sassoon, with whom he spent time convalescing from shell shock at Craiglockhart War Hospital in Edinburgh. After his recovery, Owen returned to teaching.

In 1918, when, after returning to battle, Sassoon was sent back to England from the front with a head wound, Owen felt honor-bound to "replace" Sassoon in France. In July 1918, against the advice of Sassoon and others, he returned to the fighting. In October, he was awarded the *Military Cross* for bravery. On November 4, 1918, just one week before the Armistice, while leading his men across the narrow Sambre-Oise Canal near Ors, he was shot in the head and killed. He is buried in Ors Communal Cemetery, adjacent to the canal.

Owen developed a voice that harshly rebuked war, as manifest in his famous poem *"Dulce et Decorum Est,"* from which comes the following fragment:

"Bent double, like old beggars under sacks,
Knock-kneed, coughing like hags, we cursed through sludge
Till in the haunting flares we turned our backs
And towards our distant rest began to trudge."

Less well known than Owen but considered nearly his equivalent in poetic talent was Isaac Rosenberg. A short-statured bronchitic who returned from a period of cure in South Africa in 1915 to enlist to support his mother, he was killed (probably by a sniper) at the end of a night patrol, just as dawn was breaking, in Fampoux, near the Somme River, on April 1, 1918. Rosenberg was also an artist. He attended the Slade School of Fine Art, rubbing shoulders there with many notable artists. His self-portraits hang in the National Portrait Gallery in London and in the Tate Britain. Some consider Rosenberg's poem *"The Break of Day in the Trenches"* to be the greatest poem of the war. In it he carries on a conversation with a rat that has graced his hand in the trench, he accusing it of also befriending Germans. A portion of that poem follows:

"What quaver, what heart aghast?
Poppies whose roots are in men's veins
Drop, and are ever dropping.."

Charles Hamilton Sorley died at age 20, already a Captain. Born in Aberdeen, the son of a professor of moral philosophy, Sorley was highly intelligent. Educated like Sassoon at Marlborough College, Oxford, he soon went to Germany and studied there at the University of Jena until the time of the war. He returned to England, enlisted and was in France as a lieutenant by May 1915. With only five months to live, he built a creative portfolio of poems. His brilliant career ended on October 13, 1915 when a sniper shot him in the head at the old coal-mining town of Hulluch, during the Battle of Loos. Grave detail crews discovered a poem on his corpse that he had recently written. It became his most famous: *"When You See Millions of the Mouthless Dead."* An excerpt follows:

"Then scanning all the o'ercrowded mass, should you
Perceive one face that you loved heretofore,

It is a spook. None wears the face you knew.
Great death has made all his for evermore."

Poet Edward Thomas was 39, nearly twice as old as Sorley, when he was killed in a concussive shell blast at the Battle of Arras on April 9, 1917, shortly after he arrived in France. Born in Lambeth on the south side of London's Thames River, he was educated at St. Paul's School and at Lincoln College, Oxford. He married early and made his living by the pen. Though prolific in his reviews, critiques, biographies and descriptions of countryside travel, he was not famous. It was only when visiting Dymock, in Gloucestershire, during which he became acquainted with Robert Frost that he was convinced (by Frost) to consider poetry as the amplifier of his voice. Sitting over a Smithwick's Ale under the nautical wheel in the *Beauchamps Arms* pub, Frost leaned into him and bade him thrust his words forth in rhyme.

Thomas heeded the advice. He became a prolific writer of poetry that was descriptive of the English countryside and England's cultural ethos. While he had the opportunity to follow Frost and his family on their return to America, guilt plagued Thomas and he enlisted in the Artist Rifles in 1915. His short tenure in France is why, although he is considered a Great War poet, his work is rarely descriptive of battle. However, in *"Rain,"* he anticipates it, as seen in this fragment of his verse:

"Rain, midnight rain, nothing but the wild rain
On this bleak hut, and solitude, and me
Remembering again that I shall die
And neither hear the rain nor give it thanks
For washing me cleaner than I have been
Since I was born into this solitude."

Oddly enough, Dr. John McCrae was not included in this book of Great War poets, though he also perished during the war.

In reading further, I saw that this was due to the restriction of its content to those English poets who had been specially commemorated with a slate plaque in Poet's Corner in Westminster Abbey, London on November 11, 1985. What the criteria for acceptance into this elite group were, I do not know. It seems odd that the full Commonwealth troops (including Canadians, like McCrae) were not considered equal to the British, given their similar sacrifices. However, in addition to those British who perished during the war, the plaque is dedicated to war survivors Richard Aldington, Laurence Binyon, Edmund Blunden, Wilfrid Gibson, Robert Graves, Ivor Gurney, David Jones, Robert Nichols, Herbert Read and Siegfried Sassoon. Inscribed on the stone is Wilfred Owen's *"Preface"* to his poems:

"My subject is War, and the pity of War. The Poetry is in the pity."

It seems ironic that the only member of the Great War poets who remained alive and attended the placement ceremony was Robert Graves.

I looked at the time. And at the beer. And at the breadbasket.

The latter two were empty but the former gave me a surplus forty-five minutes. It was 7:15. Don't ask me why an otherwise purely objective, insensitive and taciturn fellow like me would put pen to napkin in those remaining minutes, but I did, resulting in the following poem:

The War

I joined out of loyalty
To that full sense of Empire
That bid me train hard and harsh
To meet the enemy, strong and well

When I met him I found
He was none other than me,
Afraid, yet equally able.
Waiting for the telling event.

We paused as we looked
At one another in our grand garb.
He aimed and I aimed
And we shot, across the wild heather.

One of us died. I know not who.
Though I continue to practice
In London. Amongst the few
Who really know.

I called for the waiter and paid my bill as I tucked the napkin into my shirt pocket, hoping against hope that grave detail crews would not discover it. I loosened Max from the grip of the wrought iron fence surrounding the patio and slowly pedaled across the square toward Meensestraat, which guides one to the Menin Gate from the west.

Immediately, I could tell that the evening event would be well attended.

There were perhaps a thousand people milling about the Menin Gate already. I rode as close as possible to its entrance and realized that there would be no room inside for Max. Looking about, I saw that there was an outside stairway that led up to the old ramparts of the city, which overlook the southeastern moat. I wrestled Max up the stairs. Nearby, across from a small monument to Indian Commonwealth troops who had perished in the war, there stood another of the small shrines I had seen soon after riding out of Zeebrugge on my first day in Belgium. I padlocked Max and my saddlebags to it as best I could and hurried to be with the dense crowd that was hugging the walls of the Gate to witness the entire ceremony.

The Mayor of Ypres stood among a group of persons who were clearly wreath-laying guests, Helen and James among them. All traffic through the Gate had been stopped. Suddenly, at its eastern entrance, a uniformed group of buglers assembled. All went quiet with the first sounding of their horns. They played the famous British military refrain *"The Last Post"* to its haunting conclusion. As it echoed through the great hall of the Gate, onto whose light stone walls 56,000+ names of the lost had been carefully inscribed, I noticed that I had been pushed by the crowd directly in front of Panel Ten. I looked up and saw carved in the stone the name of McCrae's great friend Alexis Helmer.

As I turned back to the central ceremony, I watched as groups of persons carrying poppy wreaths walked to the staircase entrance to an observance alcove, above which was inscribed the words:

Ad Majorem Dei Gloriam

Here are recorded names
Of officers and men who fell
In Ypres Salient but to whom

The fortune of war denied
The known and honoured burial
Given to their comrades
In death.

James and Helen were the last to lay their wreaths. They took their time in the alcove, time that was respected by all. After they emerged and were situated once again near the Mayor, the buglers played *"Reveille"* to end the ceremony. The crowd paused momentarily, and then began to disintegrate into small clusters, like shell fragments taking unpredictable courses to their next destinations. I lost James and Helen in the departing crowd and reached for my cell phone to call them.

Just then it rang.

Chapter 15. The Summons

"Nigel?"

I immediately knew it was Wouter.

"We need you back here as soon as possible. Please don't question me now. Meet me at De Salient. I believe a crime has been committed, and we need your help."

I explained that I could ride the ten kilometers back to Passchendaele on Max faster than a car could retrieve me and so I went to retrieve Max from the shrine, wondering.

Chapter 16: A Perplexing Ride

Crime? Now there was a theatre in which I could find comfort.

I finally reached Max and fumbled with his lock, whose combination I eventually plugged in - the reliable 12 15 19 20 combination that I had owned since I bought Max's lock at Haig's Cyclery. "Where do these numbers come from," I thought. The universe is full of meaning - but these locks? I was clearly frantic. I had no idea what had happened in Passchendaele but I knew that I had to alert *The Ramparts* that I would not be staying overnight and Helen and James that I could not meet for dinner.

The call to *The Ramparts* went easily. A delightful young woman who I am sure was in black and wearing a form fitting apron and emitting bright but not overbearing perfume as she leaned over to hear me registered my news. The call to James and Helen?

Not so well.

They were both in tears when I called and let them know that I had been summoned back to Passchendaele for police work. They were barely able to contain themselves as they expressed how powerful the Menin Gate ceremony had been for them. By then, I was riding up Lange Torhoutstraat on the east side of Ypres and lost their signal, hoping that they understood and that we would at some time be back in touch again.

As I rode, I thought how peculiar it is to be sharply summoned to places under circumstances when one is not personally responsible for causative events. I think it must be the way that a surgeon feels when called in to care for yet another unfortunate. There is first a sense of heroism. Then there is a sense of responsibility. Finally, there is the capacity for mental distance, logic's great patron. Why did Wouter call *me*? I wondered as I pedaled Max hard and steadily on Kalfvaart to the junction with Brugseweg. As dusk loomed, I began to sense that my afternoon Boezinges wanted to leave me, so I pulled over, leaned Max against a tree and stepped into the brush near an L- shaped pond to relieve myself.

During those obligatory few moments, I looked up and over the pond to see the looming buildings of the brightly lit Jan Yperman Hospital. Then, on the pond just in front of me, in one of the reflected rays of the hospital's lights, I saw something moving - and it was coming toward me. As I swiftly buttoned up, I saw that it was only a duck, but a brazen one. It was a male Tufted Duck, a type that I often saw on English ponds.

He came within two meters of where I stood in the brush. He was clearly aware of me, yet seemed unafraid.

We gazed upon one another for a moment, and then he turned to take advantage of the hospital's lights to fully exhibit himself. He was dark black except for bright white sides, a blue-gray beak and tiny, intensely yellow eyes. Of course, he also had the jaunty rearward parabolic tuft of feathers issuing several centimeters from the back of his head that gave him his name. Once he was certain that I had taken in his plumage fully, he tipped face first into the water and dove. I waited for a minute or two, but he did not reemerge.

I stepped back to Max and resumed my ride.

I pedaled past the acute right turn just beyond the A19 highway to Roeselarestraat, heading northeast. Whether it was his plumage or his demeanor, the Tufted Duck haunted me on the remainder of my ride. The Tufted Duck, it seemed to me, symbolized so much of the meaning of the Great War. Black and white issues. Blue and gray uniforms. A little yellow cowardice. Arrogant plumage. And finally, immersion. I wondered, as I rode in the twilight, if he had ever surfaced.

Of course, in the last bit of my ride, my thoughts shifted to the unknown situation that I was about to face at De Salient. As a seasoned investigator, I knew not to speculate at this point, so I might bring objectivity to whatever the scene in Passchendaele might be. Still, I wondered, as I rode, what might have happened. I thought first of theft. Then of fraud, which at least required a shred of creativity. Then, aah, perhaps treason? But why here? And why now? Then? The unthinkable: murder. But who and why? Especially in this apparently very well adjusted countryside.

Night had fallen as I entered, *De Salient*, so bright with all of its inside lights on. It appeared even more welcoming than on my first visit. As before, all of its trench-cubicles were filled with eating and drinking conversationalists, but this time I sensed a quieter tone, and I definitely felt observed. After all, information in Belgium travels faster informally than anywhere on earth. As I walked past the bar, the

Canadian General - Bartender had a grave expression on his face as he passed me a Passendale ale and gestured with one hand toward the large room in the back. He took my saddlebags and handed me a key for room 0, upstairs.

"Don't ask any questions in the hallway," he said.

Now I began to worry.

I strode down the long hallway, Passendale in hand. At the end, I reached the big planning room where I knew Wouter would be sitting. I came around the corner and saw his great shock of and his worry. He was a big, dark man gone pale. I immediately knew how this would affect the many men about him. There was beer on the table, I observed, but there was also a profound intensity in that room.

Something major had just happened.

Those present were in the first throes of finding out the perpetrator(s) and the reason(s). As I entered, Wouter closed the heavy door behind me. Sitting in the room were four anxious members of the Belgian Bomb Disposal Battalion. Each had a glass of beer in his hand but few sips were being taken. Wouter introduced me to them all, including Korporaal Koen Van Aalst, who held a small plastic bag containing a solid white object measuring about 3x3 cm. Wouter explained how, just after 3 PM, the Big Bertha shell at Lark Farm had apparently spontaneously exploded and that Paula Van de Poel and the Belgian Bomb Disposal Battalion Commander, 1ste Sergeant-Majoor Geert de Smet, had been killed.

Wouter continued: "I arrived at the farm within twenty minutes. By then, the Bomb Disposal Battalion was on the scene, searching for the victims, securing the area and preparing for a search of the blast cavity. Thijs Van de Poel had been plowing in the rear field and had been blown from his tractor and was essentially unhurt, but we were worried about a concussion. Their maid, Marijke, had been struck multiple times by flying glass fragments and would require medical attention, so we had an ambulance take her to Jan Yperman hospital for care. We had another transport Thijs there for observation.

"All of the guests had checked out, and no new guests had arrived, so we simply took precautions to be sure that no gas shells had been detonated or were leaking. We also cordoned off Lark Farm and posted instructions redirecting new arrivals to other nearby bed and breakfast businesses, which we had informed of the situation. Korporaal van Aalst then suited up, entered the blast crater and found multiple unexploded shells of smaller caliber than the Big Bertha. He was in the process of loading these into an extraction crate when he noticed something unusual. I will leave it to him to describe to you what he saw."

I turned to him. Korporaal van Aalst had a very quiet voice. Clearly stressed by what had happened that afternoon, he calmly related the following: "As I collected the last of a set of perhaps eleven rusted weapon canisters from the sides and bottom of the crater, my boot moved aside a toeful of newly fallen dirt, exposing this." With that, he held up the plastic bag containing the white object, then handed it to me to view more closely. As he did, he said, "I instinctively knew it was an object that did not belong in the crater. Unlike everything else that had been buried for a century, it was not rusted. Besides, it looks like it has a plastic cover - and there was no plastic in WWI. In addition, it appeared to have been flattened, suggesting to me that it was somewhere near the blast point. I was simply not sure why it was there, so I picked it up with gloves and put it into the specimen bag."

With a nod of his great, bushy head, Wouter dismissed the battalion with thanks and sympathy for the loss of one of their own. The Battalion members then moved to another part of *De Salient* to finish their beer, leaving Wouter and me alone behind the closed door.

I looked at the object in the bag very carefully and came to my own conclusion as to its origins. However, I wanted to see what Wouter was mulling over, so I asked him what he made of the finding.

Wouter cleared his throat, took a sip of his beer and said: "Well, Nigel, I initially had the Bomb Disposal Battalion team come to *De Salient* in order to calm their nerves after having lost their colleague Geert and their friend, Paula. Not the first time for them, you know - but it is never easy.

"When we arrived, Van Aalst took me aside and showed me his finding and how he came upon it. I began to look at the object carefully. As you can see when you look at it, it has a corner that has been torn off, but it is otherwise square and flat. One side has a metallic band with what appear to be contact points. In addition, when we rubbed a little of the accompanying dirt over the surface, part of a serial number came into view - CN C 83621 is visible, but the rest of it was lost with the torn corner. I took photographs of the object through the bag and sent them to our lab in Moorslede to be analyzed.

"The team there applied complex image analysis software to the object and also checked the database of the Interpol International Serial Number Crime Archive System. They determined that it was a battery from a cell phone. Not only that, they determined that the unique initial sequence of the serial number indicated that it had to have been from a lot that was sold in Alberta, Canada. Then, they asked me if I would take end-on photographs of the metallic strip and I did. Within half an hour, they indicated that they had initially been unable to match the image of the strip to known cell phone batteries but ten minutes later they called me back with an interesting finding.

"They asked me to look at the metallic strip with a magnifying glass and confirm if I saw two thin strands of an additional silvery material on the strip, perpendicular to the strip itself. When I had the owner of *De Salient* lend me a magnifier I could immediately see two rough crossing strips of metallic material on the base strip. They then did a digital subtraction of these zones on the images and deconvoluted the twisted metallic strip and requeried the database. They were able to verify that the metallic band matched that of a Canadian cell phone battery variety that had been sold in great numbers by CanAlb Communications of Alberta. Tomorrow, when we are at the lab, we will perform verification tests to determine if the transverse metallic strips represent solder, which I suspect. But first, we will perform a thorough analysis of the DNA that is attached to the device. That's why we haven't opened the bag."

"Very intriguing," I said. "But why did you call me in?"

"Well, Nigel, as a guest of the bed and breakfast who was seen leaving just hours before the blast, you are technically a suspect." He smiled, ran his hand through his hair, took on a more serious tone and said. "Do you recall when we worked the London bombings together? What was your core expertise in the study of those crimes?"

"Improvised Explosive Devices triggered by cell phones."

"When I saw the crossing lines of what I assume to be solder on the contact points, I remember the fragment of a cell phone battery that we retrieved from that blown double-decker bus, which had a similar appearance. So I immediately thought of you as someone who could help. Besides, this is a small place, and I am going to need the input of an objective outsider as I begin the process of investigation."

I nodded in agreement as he pushed a pad of paper over to me and said, "If you agree, I will draw up the proper documents that make your engagement official but for now, can we work on an investigation plan together? I have already obtained a warrant from the magistrate to search Lark Farm. My team from Moorslede is there now, obtaining samples for DNA analysis and searching for whatever other evidence they may find. Lark Farm will be under guard until we resolve this. Can you please jot down your immediate thoughts while I request some supper for each of us? You look hungry. And thirsty," he said, as he exited the room.

In the fifteen minutes that Wouter was absent, ordering our meal and coordinating the team, the door opened only once. The Canadian General delivered a pitcher of Passendale, sternly doffed his cap and retreated, the door closing tight.

During that time, I drew on my experience in London and drafted an immediate Plan of Analysis that included the following:

1. Identification of all guests, owners and staff that had been at Lark Farm in the past month, particularly those from Alberta. I immediately thought of James and Helen and her lost cell phone but tried not to rush to judgment. I also thought about the conversation they had had with Thijs as they paid and departed from Lark Farm.

2. Cell phone numbers for all of the above. Cell phone outgoing and incoming records for each, including frequency and timing.

3. Contact CanAlb Communications to identify the remainder of the serial number and to zero in the site at which the phone had been sold - and perhaps to whom it had been sold.

I then had a few remaining minutes to consider the scenario. If the Big Bertha shell had been turned into an IED, the following had to have occurred:

A: The Big Bertha shell had to have been discovered in place: it was too large and heavy to have been transported to Lark Farm in broad daylight.

B: A detonation mechanism had to have been at hand.

C: A person skilled in the art of IED manufacture had to have had access to the shell for a long enough period of time to be able to put the mechanism in place.

D: Soldering and other tools needed to be available to construct the detonation mechanism.

E: In most cases, the cell phone would have had to be disabled until just before the blast, to prevent accidental, premature discharge.

As I thought over these elements of the case, Wouter and the Canadian General returned, arms heavy with bread, cheese and steaming plates of roast duck, carrots and mashed potatoes, swimming in a rich, rust-brown gravy.

"This will replenish the weary cyclist," Wouter said, as he tucked in his napkin as a bib and began his meal. I put the pad aside and took the time, in the Belgian way, to simply enjoy the meal and the company. It was delicious. I had traveled eighty kilometers on Max during the day and needed the sustenance. As we ate, we spoke about the places I had visited, about my eerie blowout that coincided with the time of the explosion, and about the ghosts and the birds that had haunted me all day.

Wouter was not surprised by any of it. "This is, after all, a haunted place, Nigel. What did you expect?"

With that, he took his last bite and pulled my pad over to him. He took out his reading glasses and ticked his way down the list. When he was done, he picked up his phone and called to his detail at Lark Farm. He spoke quickly: "Tell the men to retrieve fingerprints, toothbrushes, hairbrushes, computers, guest books and any telephone equipment that lies there. Have them catalog it all, as usual, by place of origin and let's all meet at the lab in Moorslede at nine am, sharp. Also, put two guards at the hospital to watch over Thijs Van de Poel and the maid, Marijke."

Wouter called the lab and asked the evening shift to obtain the answers to #s 1-4 in the above list and said that we would meet with them in the morning for a report. Then we drank a nightcap whiskey at the bar.

I tossed and turned in my bed. Before I eventually slept, I sent Emil an email, indicating that I would be extending my stay in Belgium, as I had been invited to participate in an important investigation. I also wrote him a narrative of my full day's events, with all of their emotional impact. I even transcribed my poem from the napkin and sent it to him. If anyone would understand, I was sure that Emil would.

Finally, I slept.

I awoke at six to a gray day. As so often happens when I wake up in a strange bed, I found myself disoriented. A heavy red blanket was down around my legs, indicating that I had been doing a bit more tossing and turning in the night. My wallet was on the nightstand, along with my wedding ring. I wondered why I had taken it off, even as heavy congeners of Scotch suffused the air around me. The lead-framed window, hidden slightly by intricate lace pull curtains, was frugal with the light it allowed to enter. The wallpaper depicted artistically displayed bayonets, and my slacks were in disarray on the floor. My saddlebags were on the desk and opened only to the extent that a toothbrush could have emerged, somehow, late last night.

With a groan that coupled the agonies of a hangover with those of a long bicycle ride by an untrained body, I arose. When I saw myself in the mirror, I thought "No wonder Lois left me," and entered the bath to shower, shave and put things marginally right. As I did, I heard Wouter clattering about, next door. After cleaning up, I sat for a bit with a coffee in a flimsy cup after the in-room brewer sputtered its last. I took notes.

Wouter and I met downstairs at 7:30 for a full Belgian breakfast. The array had nothing on Paula's Lark Farm offering, but hardened investigators that we were, we tried everything and sated ourselves. It promised to be a big day.

As we stepped outside, I checked on Max to be sure that he was secure. We then rode in Wouter's cruiser over the ridge to Moorslede. The radio crackled nonsensically, as often happens in police vehicles. Something about a boat being stolen on the encircling canals of Bruges. The ride was brief, we conversed little and we arrived on time.

The entire staff was there, waiting to provide us their collective report on the evening's findings.

Chapter 17. Moorslede and Lark Farm

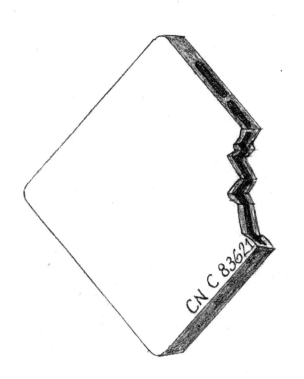

Before I discuss the team and their findings, let me share an image of the site.

There is a ridge just on the western edge of Moorslede that hides it from Passchendaele. As we drove over the ridge, there lay before us a string of modest homes on the street leading into the town center. About halfway down on the left hand side, across from a cornfield that was raised above the road by a few feet, laid a gleaming building, all of glass. Even from afar, we could see everyone in the building, all actively engaged in his or her work. The glass was framed by blue-grey metalwork that seemed indistinct until we were close. Then, I realized that the metalwork was in the form of scrolls or helices. The glass took on odd tints and when viewed at the precisely correct angle exhibited arrays of multicolored dots. The doors to the building had handles like gentle Vs facing in opposite directions so that when the doors were closed, an "X" was formed. The name, Moorslede Center for Molecular Forensics, was prominently displayed on the right hand door. As we entered the lobby, I noticed a light display that began with one blue light that became two, then four, and then eight, then sixteen and so on until the lobby was drenched in blue.

I asked Wouter about the architecture, which stood out so starkly from that of its neighborhood. Wouter stood in the midst of the ever-expanding blue lights and said: "When the European Union funded this operation, they co-funded the Department of Architecture at the University of Leuven to design the building. The site, oddly enough, was selected by the neighbors themselves, who appealed to the EU to place something grand and modern at the former site of a German field hospital from the Great War. If you exit the back of the building, you will notice a graveyard there, which is why the lot had always remained vacant after the war.

"I have always found the symbolism of the building to be important. The metal framework, of course, represents the double helix of DNA. The door handle symbolizes the chromosome and the glass shell, while appearing transparent, actually symbolizes the analysis of gene expression, as you saw when you viewed the glass at the right angle to see the results of a gene expression microarray. The transparency not only suggests that through genetic analysis we can see through many problems, it also lets me know if the team is working, when I come over the ridge in my cruiser." With that, Wouter winked.

We entered.

Their first report was that both Thijs and Marijke had vanished from the hospital.

I watched Wouter as he absorbed this and was impressed to see his calm and his focus. The report indicated that the two policemen who were sent to guard Marijke and Thijs at the hospital had found their rooms empty and had spent the night scouring the area around Jan Yperman Hospital, trying to find them.

Earlier that day, Marijke had spent two to three hours in the emergency room having tiny shards of glass removed from her face, neck and hands. Fortunately, though it had been a warm day, she had been wearing a heavy woolen coat at the time of the blast. When it was removed and shaken, glass shards tinkled from it onto the floor like sleet in an ice storm. She was then admitted to a wardroom for observation.

Thijs, upon arriving at the hospital, had had a full neurological evaluation, a cervical spine X-ray series and a baseline head CT scan, which was read as normal. He, too, had been admitted for observation, in the room next to Marijke's. The only additional test, a blood count, was performed an hour after his admission. It remained normal, ruling out internal bleeding. Despite the fact that his tests were normal, his nurse indicated that he seemed a bit "off," which she thought might simply be the effect of grief, though oddly, he never mentioned the loss of his wife.

Wouter called the two tired policemen, sent them home to rest and assigned two more to the case. "Check to see that no cars and no bicycles have been stolen at Jan Yperman and start a thorough search in Ypres, itself," he directed. He then turned to the staff, removed the plastic bag and its contents from his pocket and said "How long will it take to run a Polymerase Chain Reaction and the Moorslede Short Tandem Repeat Protocol on a wiping from this battery, and can we get prints from it, as well?" A sound-looking male senior technician in a white lab coat stepped forth, took the bag and said "We'll have it all for you by eleven am."

Wouter then turned to me and explained: "While PCR will expand any DNA on the battery for analysis, the Moorslede Protocol will allow us to distinguish new DNA from old. Normally, Short Tandem Repeats (STR) from highly conserved intron areas are measured in four to five base segments. However, since we have so much degraded DNA in all the soil in Flanders from war dead, we run our Protocol targeting six nucleotide sequences and do a comparison to the same process targeting four and five nucleotide sequences. When we see a sharp step off in STR quantity between the sets, we opt for the data from the Moorslede Protocol, as it is more likely to target fresh DNA, despite some problems it introduces in the PCR methodology." I nodded, recognizing the distinct difference from the methods we used at the Yard at the time of the London bombings. Wouter had created a nice innovation that suited his geography.

Wouter then turned to another technician and asked "What about the biological material from Lark Farm?" An equally astute looking technician, this time an unusually tall, full-faced woman with black hair and green eyes and a tiny mole on her left temple stepped forward and read from last night's police search report:

"The team was able to retrieve toothbrushes, hair brushes and hairs from the rooms of the Van de Poels, Marijke, the MacCormicks, Mr. Hendricks – " she nodded respectfully to me as she said this – "and several other guests. They were also able to obtain the guest log with cell phone numbers, cell phone numbers for Thijs and Paula, the Lark Farm main telephone and its attached answering machine. Fortunately, the password for the answering machine was taped onto its underside, a common practice, it seems, so we were able to retrieve a list of all of its calls and its present setup state. We have performed PCR to scale up the DNA signature on all of the materials we received and are in the process of performing the standard and Moorslede Protocol STR analyses, which we expect to have completed in two hours."

She went on. "We also woke the magistrate to obtain a warrant to retrieve all of the suspects' cell phone activities – " once again, she nodded respectfully to me – "and the telephone activity at Lark Farm, itself. We are in the process of pulling a map of all of that activity together and should have it for you in an hour or so."

I was impressed by their focus on their work and the high speeds with which they were able to analyze complex biological material. We were certainly not so technically up to date at the Yard.

"Thank you all," Wouter said. "I'm sure that it has been a long night for all of you."

As the team returned to its duties, Wouter poured me a steaming mug of coffee from an ornate urn that sat on a side table in the conference room. Each mug had a very interesting design. The first quarter of the ceramic at the base was an umber color. At various points around the mugs, double helices emerged from this base layer and, twisting together, tapered upward to what appeared to be a bright blue sky. They were beautiful to see.

And the coffee was excellent.

As we sat together, I spoke with Wouter about the MacCormicks from Calgary, Helen's lost cell phone, their odd conversation with Thijs the day before and their hearty appetites. I also explained that I had James's cell phone number and could probably reach them, most likely in Dunquerque or Normandy.

"Do you think they will make a run for it if we simply call them?" Wouter asked.

"No," I said. "I will simply tell them that I've found Helen's cell phone and that I would like to take them to lunch to compensate for missing them last evening at *The Ramparts*. And I won't take 'No' for an answer. Then, if they run, we will have a better understanding of them. Let's notify the police in Normandy and in Paris, too, just to be on the safe side. Their car's license plate number will be in the guest log from Lark Farm." Wouter called in an assistant to take care of notifying the French police as I put in the call to James.

When James answered, I could tell that he was in a thoughtful mood, not his normal, jocular self. "It is good to hear from you Nigel. Yes, we understand about last night. We had a good meal at *The Ramparts* and slept soon afterwards. We were up at five, drove to Dunquerque for a look and are now walking on Juno Beach in Normandy. Many of my father's friends served in the 3d Canadian Infantry when they landed here. Thankfully, none were killed."

I replied: "You certainly get off to a good start on the day, James. Let me tell you why I am calling. I believe I have found Helen's cell phone and would like to return it to you. If you can run back up here to

Passchendaele, I promise to buy you lunch at *The Arrow* or better, *De Salient* and send you off properly to Paris. It's the least I could do after standing you up last evening."

I used every bit of my formal British accent to give the request weight. James conferred with Helen for a moment, then agreed to return. "The phone plan is restrictive, as you know - it really is better for Helen to continue to use that phone. Besides, we have grown fond of enjoying meals with you, Nigel. We can be there by noon."

"Let's meet at *De Salient* on Grenadiersstraat in Passchendaele," I said. "You will know it because Max will be outside, beaming his usual bright redness to the world."

James laughed and said "See you then. But I warn you - Helen will be thirsty."

Wouter then did something interesting. He opened his laptop, connected it to a projector that illuminated the opposite wall and opened a mind-mapping program. In the center node, he typed the word "Murder."

"Pretty frank, that Wouter," I thought. Then, in a series of child nodes, he wrote the words "Suspects," "Motives" and finally "Methods." Beneath the 'Suspects' node, he then listed the following names:

Helen
James
Nigel
Koen
Marijke
Other Bomb Disposal Personnel
Other British Guests
Belgian Couple (Guests)
Paula
Geert
Mrs. De Smet
Neighbor
Thijs

Then, under the 'Motives' node, he typed the following:

Jealousy
Revenge
Money
Hate

Under the 'Methods' node, he listed only one item:

Knowledge of cell-phone triggered IED construction

Wouter asked me if I had any additional input and I indicated that I thought his lists were quite complete, save for the inclusion of his name on the suspect list. He lifted his bushy head, smiled his Belgian smile and added his name to the list. Then, he printed out the map in two copies, gave me one, tucked the other in his shirt pocket and said: "Nigel, we have a good two hours before the test results are back and the MacCormicks arrive. Why don't we have a look at Lark Farm together?" This was exactly what I had hoped we would do next. As I rose, Wouter called one of his staff members and instructed him to ascertain the whereabouts of the Belgian couple, the British guests, Mrs. De Smet and the neighbors at 3pm yesterday. He also asked for the telephone records that had been pulled together thus far, so we could study them a bit later. Then we stepped out of *De Salient* into brilliant sunshine. Max, I noticed as we slipped into Wouter's cruiser, was comfortably sunbathing. As we drove past, the sun reflected from the handlebar in a strobe flash.

I could swear that Max was winking at me.

Down the Passchendaele ridge we drove, Lark Farm visible in the distance, shattered windows, bomb crater and all. As we approached, several neighbors on bicycles were standing by the police tape, simply looking at the B&B, the farm buildings and the destruction that the bomb had wrought. The guard let Wouter through the police tape and into the driveway, where he stepped from the vehicle and took a report from the guard.

I took the opportunity to do some exploring. First, I went to the edge of the bomb crater and looked into its depths, which were impressive. Large clods of dirt lay everywhere within and around the crater. Here and there, a bit of rusted metal could be seen. I instinctively looked around for any evidence of Paula Van de Poel or Geert De Smet, though I knew from the looks of the blast crater that I would find none, not even a button.

Turning to the outbuildings, I entered the one in which I had stored Max last evening. Constructed as a low-lying barn, half was devoted to tractors, tillers and other farm equipment. Beyond a separating wall in the middle of the building, however, was an entirely different sight. It was a room fitted out as a classroom in whose periphery all manner of WWI relics were displayed. Rusted guns, bullets, shell casings, complete shells, lengths of barbed wire, helmets, fragmented uniforms, cigarette cases, bayonets and swords were present, amongst other paraphernalia. I picked up one short sword, felt its heft and touched the edge of its blade with my index finger. That it had retained its edge became clear when I withdrew my finger and noticed a drop of blood. It was as if the sword had reached out and bitten me. As I replaced it in its display, I pinched the laceration until it bled no more.

In the corner of the room, there was a British flag, vintage 1918, hanging vertically, unfurled. Moving it aside slightly, I could see a wooden door behind it. Curious, I tried the handle. It was firmly locked. Traffic marks on the dirt floor suggested that it had been approached recently, so I made a note to let Wouter know about it.

I then looked through the other outbuildings and finally, completely explored the B&B building. The Ell room looked quite different with all of its windows blown in. Even its shower stall glass was shattered. Nowhere in any of the buildings could I find soldering equipment, or even the drill that would be needed to insert wires through a phone casing, items that would be needed to construct a cell phone-triggered IED.

When I returned to Wouter, he had just completed a similar tour to mine, also finding nothing unusual except the results of the blast. Just as I was about to mention the locked door in the barn, his cell phone rang. His men in Ypres were calling to tell him that there had been no sign of Marijke or Thijs at any of the restaurants or hotels in the city and that no vehicles had been reported missing. Wouter instructed them to stay on station, closed his phone, turned to me and said: "There's no sign of them."

Then, as has often happened to me in my investigative life, a subconscious hunch rose into consciousness, and I asked Wouter to follow me. We walked into the B&B and then directly to the back door. Wouter had learned from Marijke that she had been standing there when she had waved to Thijs to have him come in from his tractor to meet the Bomb Disposal Battalion, yesterday afternoon. According to Wouter, she had been thrown into the haymow, ten feet distant, at the time of the blast. I asked Wouter if I could see the telephone records, which he produced. I scanned the list of numbers, selected one and dialed it, Wouter watching me intently.

The wind was blowing gently from the northeast again as we stood in the doorway. The sun shone bright. We remained perfectly still as I heard first the ringing in my phone and then, seconds later, the gentle trill of a ringtone, calling to us from the tilled furrows, just beyond the tractor Thijs had been driving when the blast occurred.

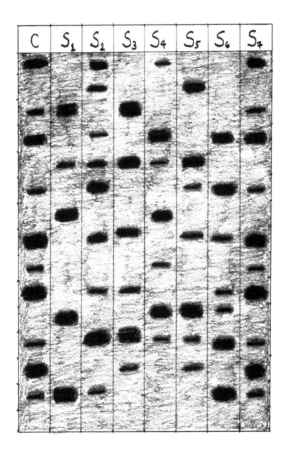

Wouter and I looked briefly at one another and then we walked, furrow by square-off furrow out into the field toward the tractor. As we approached, we saw that its Plexiglas windows had been blown in on its south side and blown out on its north, the latter serving as Thijs' exit route at the time of the blast. The direction of his exit lined up neatly with the new furrow that his body had created, perpendicular to the rest.

I called his cell phone number again to locate his phone. After two rings, Wouter found it, covered with earth, at the end of the furrow Thijs' body had made. Wouter retrieved it into an evidence bag and without a word, pressed its keys through the plastic to see the list of previous outgoing calls. The last call that had been made on the phone was to Lark Farm, at 3:10 PM yesterday.

I wondered briefly how Max's front tire had been able to sense that faraway signal.

Searching the tractor and finding nothing revealing, we stepped over the molded furrows and returned to the B&B. As we stepped through the front door, Wouter had a parting word with the guard, and we climbed into his cruiser for the ride back to Moorslede. As we rode, we discussed the relevance of the cell phone finding and the timing of Thijs' last call.

Wouter spoke first: "I would find it odd that If Thijs were involved in something criminal that he would leave his cell phone behind - that is, unless he is clever enough to have contrived a plot to make it look like he was so concerned with Paula after the blast that he would focus solely on her."

I said, "Or perhaps he didn't know that it had fallen from his pocket at the time and was simply whisked away to the hospital before he was aware of its absence. Or, he knew that we could triangulate on any calls he might make and locate him, so it would be a liability should he take it with him on the run." We were ruminating on these possibilities when we pulled into the Center for Molecular Forensics. The flashing lights in the lobby, formerly blue, were now a crimson red. We walked by them, down the entry hall, and into the main conference room.

As soon as we arrived, Wouter's assistant entered and informed us that the MacCormicks had just called, were passing by Ypres and confirmed that they would reach *De Salient* by noon. Wouter asked her to confirm with them that we would be there on time and also asked that she assemble his investigative team in the conference room immediately. As she was leaving, she also recounted how the French police had called to let Wouter know that the MacCormicks had been discreetly followed until they were just over the border into Belgium. Wouter nodded, thanked her and asked her to send those officers a special magnum of his favorite claret on his Euro, he assured me, as the team came together.

"OK, let's begin," he urged. "Let's start with the searchers for Marijke and Thijs," he said, activating the conference call console. After two rings, the hoarse sound of a police cruiser came alive over the central room amplifier. Wouter welcomed his two officers to the conference and asked: "Have you learned anything about their whereabouts?"

One of the officers replied, "They were not seen leaving the hospital, and there have been no sightings of a man and woman in the area that match their description. We have scoured Ypres and are beginning to do a circumferential search of the towns surrounding Ypres. We are in Messines at the moment."

Wouter encouraged them to continue but also to be sure that train and bus schedules and departures were known and covered by trusted stationmasters. "You can do this in a small country," he said, in an aside to me. They indicated that they had already seen to this and that there were no reports. Wouter accepted this information, asked them to stay on the line but to please, please, mute their loud cruiser phone.

The room suddenly went very quiet, in the absence of automobile engine noise.

Wouter had previously grouped his technicians into teams to handle various aspects of the investigation. He turned first to Team One, responsible for determining the whereabouts of all suspect parties at the time of yesterday's blast. Their report included the following:

The Wallonian Belgian couple was at a realtor in Zonnebeke, putting in a bid for a bungalow that they had toured just that morning.

The British guests, contacted by cell phone, were already in Munich, at a bar near the Glockenspiel. They were difficult to understand as their words were slurred. The proprietor of the bar verified that they had been there at mid afternoon yesterday, as well.

Mrs. de Smet, devastated by the news of her husband's death, was rushing back from a floral convention in Innsbruck.

The neighbors, in turn, were all seen immediately after the blast, leaving their homes and heading to the blast site on bicycles.

Wouter requested a report from Team Two, responsible for analyzing the biological material that had been obtained from Lark Farm. I really liked the way Wouter organized an investigative response. The next presenter came forward.

The tall woman with black hair, green eyes, the small mole and what I now saw were very shapely legs stepped forth to the podium. She began by listing the biological specimens the team had obtained at Lark Farm.

'First we entered all of the rooms of Lark Farm and retrieved anything of biological interest we could find. We checked the guest log to see who had stayed where, and we also entered the main house to obtain samples representative of the Van de Poel family, as a whole. We also entered Marijke's room in the B&B and took samples from dirty clothing and a hairbrush.

"When we processed all of these samples, we found that we were able to use PCR to magnify good DNA expression from each. We then ran standard and Moorslede Protocol STR analyses on each. So within the past half hour, we were ready to apply software from Interpol to do comparative analysis with the DNA that Team Three had found on the battery sample." With that, she made a humorous curtsy and exited the podium to allow the Team Three technician to hold forth.

He stood erect and thoughtful as he began. "As you can imagine, trying to trace DNA to a specific individual when an object has been exposed to the DNA of thousands in the soil of Flanders is no easy task. By first magnifying the DNA present and then filtering it using the standard and Moorslede Protocol STR analyses, we were able to identify three distinct, recent DNA signatures on the battery. So we focused specifically on these."

All members present in the room gasped slightly in anticipation of their findings.

"When we applied Interpol Comparative Bioinformatics software to the data, we were able to confirm that the modern DNA on the battery came from James MacCormick, Helen MacCormick and the maid, Marijke. We also identified the DNA of hundreds of others, though in each case, the DNA was highly fragmented and therefore old and of no use to our case. This is fairly typical of what we find when we inspect soil-contaminated samples in Flanders."

Wouter and I looked at one another and he raised a broad and bushy left eyebrow, then returned to his attention to his team.

The Team Four spokesperson then stepped forth. He and his team were responsible for the telephone records. "We spent most of our time determining who called who, when and also identifying the state of reception of each of the devices involved. First, Paula called De Smet from her cell phone three times during the day. At one point, they spoke for an hour."

Wouter grimaced. The Team Four spokesperson continued. "Second, Thijs made his only call of the day at 3:10 PM, when he called the Lark Farm main number. More on that, later. Third, Nigel's phone –" he turned to me with a slight bow of respect - "was silent during the day. Fourth, no calls were made during the day from Helen's cell phone, but James's phone registered four calls to her cell phone number in quick succession near noontime, all of which went to voicemail without ringing her phone, according to CanAlb Communications. They also indicated that until 3:09 pm, the phone had been programmed to receive no calls and at 3:09 pm it had been programmed to receive calls only from the Lark Farm main number.

"Fifth, three calls were made to Lark Farm from around the world (probably from interested guests, we surmised) between two and 3:09 PM, but none were able to connect with the main number. All of them state this on their follow-up emails to the Lark Farm account. We learned this from West Flanders Communications, with whom Lark Farm had their phone and email contracts.

"Lastly, though the answering machine was an older version, we were able to find that it had been set up at 3:09 pm to call forward any incoming calls to Helen's cell phone number."

Wouter thanked the speaker and turned to me and said: "Well, won't Thijs be surprised to learn that he killed his own wife, though perhaps inadvertently?"

I looked up at the wall and thought about the situation. Marijke had had access to everyone's rooms. Thijs had indicated to Marijke that he wished to be alerted by signal when the Bomb Disposal battalion was arriving and that he would call in to clarify the exact time that retrieval of the bomb would commence - and he had allowed others to overhear this. Marijke, on a warm day, had been wearing a long woolen coat when she had been blown into the haymow. Helen and James had been far away and had made no electronic communication with Lark Farm at the critical time.

And at the time of the blast and just beforehand, Marijke had been the only one in the B&B, as Paula had been out front with De Smet for several minutes after 3 PM.

It appeared that we had our culprit. But what was her motive? And what was Thijs's involvement, if any?

Wouter dismissed the staff; we discussed our findings on our way to the cruiser and to *De Salient*, where Helen and James, we knew, would be patiently waiting. As would be silent Max. We drove in silence. I wondered who exactly *was* this Marijke.

As we rode, I penned a note to Emil, outlining the issues in the case. I also expressed to him how wonderfully Wouter, whom he had trained, had developed as an investigator. I made it clear that as he had predicted, this experience was changing my life, bringing something alive that had been dead. I was not quite sure what, yet.

I looked forward to seeing the MacCormicks again, but not as the dissembler that I had unfortunately become.

Chapter 19. Of Foreign Wars

When we met the MacCormicks, I explained that we were going to need beer in hand before any serious discussion could take place. The Canadian General promptly fulfilled this requirement, and I introduced them to Wouter.

"The good news," I said, "Is that you are no longer suspects in a murder investigation."

They looked at one another in shock, jaws dropping.

"If that is good news, Nigel, then what is the bad news?" Helen inquired.

"Your cell phone no longer functions," I answered.

Helen and James looked at one another again, shrugged their strong Canadian shoulders and said in unison "I guess this is going to be a fascinating lunch discussion."

And it was.

When Wouter and I saw them off to Paris after lunch, we knew we had each met friends for life.

We turned to one another and we each said one word aloud, yet again: "Marijke."

We drove in silence back to the Center and met once again with the team. By then, they had obtained an Interpol report on one Marijke Radvilke, an Albanian Kosovar physician who had had an immense reputation as a surgeon before she joined the Kosovo Liberation Army and soon became a war crimes suspect in relation to illegal organ harvesting.

Wouter and I looked at one another, stunned.

Several years earlier, she had disappeared from Kosovo. A team of investigators at Interpol had periodically and surreptitiously scanned the staff directories of surgery departments throughout Europe but no one of her description had ever been seen. In addition, she had allowed her license to practice medicine to lapse. Some thought that she might have met an untimely death.

"Apparently not," Wouter said, with his characteristic understatement. "Let's take a ride," he said.

Off we went in his cruiser to Ypres, Messines, Zonnebeke, Poelcapelle, Langemarck, Poeperinge, Westrozebeke, looking everywhere for persons who might match Marijke's and Thijs's descriptions. All of Wouter's other team members were doing the same in their own vehicles. There was not a single meaningful sighting.

Late in the evening, we returned to *De Salient* for a dinner of steak with shallot sauce and crisp frites.

And many, many Passendales.

Chapter 20. Marijke

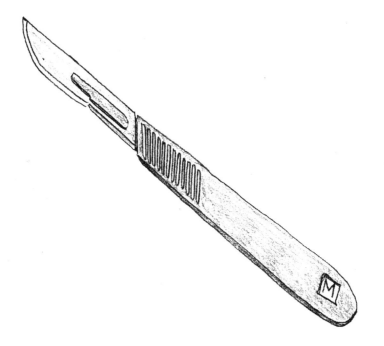

I retired to a fitful sleep that night at *De Salient*.

The sheer abundance of intelligence that we had collected on Marijke in one day was impressive and required some digesting. We were all unsettled by the fact that someone of her dark past and high skills remained on the run. We could only imagine what she had done with Thijs - unless, of course, he had taken up with her. "No," I thought, "Not Thijs." This led me to imagining the recovery of his body from the Spanbroekmoelen Crater or even the Ijser Canal.

It was one am when, tossing and turning, I stood up and went to the window, which faced onto the parking lot and the adjacent grounds of *De Salient*. The poppies in the window box blew about in the warm May night as I approached. I opened the window and stuck my head out to look to the left to see if I could see Max where he was locked up for the night.

To my surprise, his headlight was on.

I pulled on my clothing and picked my way through the night-shaded halls and stairwell of *De Salient*. I passed the empty bar and trenches and quietly slipped out the front door to the parking area. Grenadiersstraat, as expected, was completely silent. A view past it to the gently sloping valley was punctuated by the flickering outdoor lights of farmhouses, before which blew tree leaves and bushes in a blustery southwest wind. It was an ironic, peaceful beauty, given that the same flickering a century before would be from the guns. All of them. Everywhere.

When I reached Max, I noticed that his front tire was directed toward the southwest, his light shining precisely in the direction of Lark Farm. After I switched it off, I stood for quite some time looking at Lark Farm's heavy shadow, in the near distance. Then, for whatever reason, I applied the combination and unlocked Max.

I left his light off as I rode first up to the town square, then down the length of Canadalaan, past the monument and the Little Grebe's pond, taking a course from there westward toward Lark Farm.

I asked myself what I was trying to learn.

Earlier in my career, I would have been analytical about this, as if everything that drove our lives could be brought into the light of a rational consciousness. Too often over the years, I found that this approach had failed me. Instead, I learned to trust an instinct, one whose directives could not be put into words but which almost always was able to take into consideration more information, imagined and unimagined, into its conclusions. Like an aviator relying on his instruments in a cloud, I rode past dozing Belgian cattle, goats, sheep and young rows of crops along paths toward Lark Farm that I had not previously taken.

As I came near the Farm, I noticed that my approach had taken me to its far southwestern corner, near the edge of the barn. Listening to an inner voice, I set Max away from the road, beyond the drainage ditch, amongst a set of low-lying trees. At a minimum, I hoped to see if the guard was on duty at the entrance to the farm so I could ask him if he had observed anything unusual that evening. Why I approached him stealthily, though, was also not a part of conscious action.

There, in the darkness was a late model black Yugo sedan, pressed hard into the bushes, rear end first, like clay into a mold. The bushes nearby were disturbed, but I wasn't sure if their parting had been recent because it appeared that someone had been stockpiling unspent shells there.

Perhaps it was Thijs and his hoarding.

In the darkness, I witnessed what must have been a full armamentarium of WWI shells, British and German and French. There was even a Big Bertha shell standing erect, just by a seam in the building that I could determine with some careful observation was a little door. Why I did this with a massive live shell, I will never know, but with all my strength I gently and very quietly tipped it onto its side and obstructed the door.

Then, I crept around the barn to see if the guard was at his post,

As I turned the corner into the dimly lit courtyard of Lark Farm, I realized that he was not. A police cruiser sat in the far corner, but no guard was visible. As I looked about at the blown-in windows, I was saddened. I looked up at the Ell room and its forlorn curtain that waved in and out of the window where I had pleasantly sat so recently.

148

At a time like this, a man does one of two things. He either assesses the situation, determines that it is dangerous and calls in reinforcements or he, like the testosterone-addled idiot he is, goes it alone. I elected the latter. Call me foolish, but a man is all about stimulation and I was entering the force vortex of stimulation, at least as far as my instinct would take me. I slowly walked in the shadows toward the door to the barn and found the guard, slumped by a chair, breathing in a shallow fashion.

His weapon was gone.

I felt like I was in the movies.

His service walkie-talkie was still strapped to his belt, so against all policies, I took it and strapped it onto my own. I carefully walked the twenty meters to the entrance to the barn and entered the darkness therein. In the far corner, I could see a rectangle of slim light that emanated from the borders of the door that I had found to be locked and covered with a British flag during my previous barn inspection. Using the light from my smart phone, I illuminated the display of WWI artifacts and found and carefully retrieved the sword that had previously drawn my blood and two long strands of German barbed wire - the type with long barbs, the better to eviscerate a soldier running in No-Man's Land.

I didn't slow my walk. I didn't creep. I went right to the door and tried to open it.

It was locked.

Shrugging away this slight delay, I took the sword, pressed it gently into the lock escapement, levered it, and the door opened. The wind and the banging it created around the barn may have masked the sound of my entry but I didn't know - and at that point I didn't care. As the door opened, I saw the most uncommon sight in Flanders.

The steps to a basement.

Now why, in this place of fragile drainage, where a hundred thousand men had been sucked into lethal mud a few feet deep would anyone build a basement?

The stairs to the basement were made of spent shell casings and the walls of the basement depicted battle scenes that featured the old Lark Farm in the background. There was a bright light around the corner, but the stairs were not lit at all. I stepped carefully down, hearing an odd rustling and moaning in the room that was filled with light.

Now, in my years of investigation, I have often found myself in a defining moment. However, none was so defining as the moment when I stepped into the lit room at the bottom of the stairs.

There I stood, sword in one hand, two strands of barbed wire in the other, gazing upon a surgical operation.

There, under a bright portable lamp, a man lay face down upon a table, his legs and arms flung below him like straw. His back was painted brown with Betadine disinfectant and makeshift drapes enclosed a limited operating zone on his left flank. A small, thin woman in surgical garb had just made an incision below his lowest rib and was securing bleeders with hemostats. I watched for a moment and saw her swift hands performing their skillful act, just as she had done with the herring, recently.

It was Marijke.

In the microsecond that I had to take it all in, I recalled what a Guy's Hospital surgeon had once told me was the ultimate insult that an observer could impose upon an operating surgeon.

"I wouldn't do it that way." I said aloud.

As I uttered this, Marijke, that bundle of nerves, spun around and stared for a brief moment, then rushed for a side table where lay a syringe of uncertain content. And a gun.

Contrary to my combined British and my former wife's impression of my seemingly passive nature, I was not about to be either injected with an unknown substance or shot. Deep within me, my amygdala signaled my limbic system to act, which triggered my pituitary gland to release an active agent that set my adrenal glands afire and thence my muscles and intensely focused remainder of my mind. As Marijke reached for her deadly instruments, I took the heft of the sword in hand, rotated it to its non-cutting side and brought it down upon her outstretched arms, sparing her the sharp blade that had caught me unaware the day before.

The back of the blade struck her forearms at the midpoints of ulna and radius and cleanly fractured each, left and right, making her forearms and hands mere semaphores of agony. As she stood, astonished, I stepped forward and encircled her midsection with one length of barbed wire, twisting it tightly in her back. She tried to flee toward the secret exit door, and I allowed her to do so, knowing it was blocked by the Big Bertha shell. When she realized the door would not budge, she came back into the room, kicking and screaming in a crude Balkan screed. It was easy to spin her about by her surgical gown, flip her onto the ground and encircle her ankles with the second length of barbed wire.

Thus ciliced, she became calm, staring at me with beady eyes.

I looked over at the man on the table. It was Thijs. He was still breathing in a labored, shallow fashion.

"Dr. Radvilke," I said. "What made you abandon your Oath of Hippocrates?"

She cursed at me as she looked at her useless arms and said: "I must compliment you, Nigel - your hands were swifter than my own." Her head lay adjacent to a cooler filled with ice. I knew the view from my hospital days: she had been trying to harvest Thijs's kidney - or kidneys. The question was - why?

I felt in my pocket for the guard's walkie-talkie, which I knew had a recording function, and switched it on.

I knelt beside her as she struggled with her pain and asked, "Why did you do it, Marijke?"

As she struggled in and out of painful consciousness, I watched her face carefully, as an Investigator does. I could immediately sense that for some reason she was stalling for time. So I played her. Waiting to see why.

"Nigel," she said, taking on a feigned friendly air. "I grew up a dutiful little girl in Kosovo, daughter of Albanian parents. We lived in a little town called Ksro, where we were very happy until I was at the University of Prishlatar. Then, the ethnic cleansing began. The Serbs wanted us all out of Kosovo, despite that fact that we represented the majority of the population and had contributed so much to the culture of the region. My parents were pacifists and went along with the changes that were occurring but one night in 1998, some Serb activists poisoned our town well with Orellanine mushroom poison."

"Orellanine?" I asked.

"Yes," she said, wincing as she shifted in the wire's embrace.

"It is a mushroom derivative that poisons the kidneys irreversibly, but it takes several weeks to do so. As a result, we were never able to track down the perpetrator. My brother Vladic and I were the only residents of the village who did not lose their kidney function. I was away in medical school, and he was running a logistics office for an Albanian shipping company along the Adriatic coast. An entire dialysis center had to be set up in Ksro, at an untenable cost to the local population. The only recourse was to find a way to provide kidney transplants to the population, especially to the children.

"As you can imagine, it was an impossible situation. There was no money, and there were no organs. We became infected with the same hatred of the Serbs that our forbears had felt, and we as a village were bent on revenge. We as a people, you may know, never forgive a slight to our families."

Her eyes flashed as she said this.

"As the Kosovo War wound down in 1999, the United Nations forces allowed the Kosovo Liberation Army, composed of ethnic Albanians, to maintain public order in the outer villages of Kosovo. At that time, the KLA held hundreds of Serbian prisoners of war. By then, I had been trained as a surgeon and was practicing at the University of Prishlatar."

That explained the deft hands. Thijs moaned and then returned to somnolence.

"My practice consisted of the usual war-related amputations, and reconstructions. There really was no transplant service at the hospital but I had had such training in a world tour of transplant centers two years prior, including at the University in Istanbul, where I established strong collegial relationships. I did all I could to leverage these relationships for my fellow villagers. Until then, despite what had happened in my village, I tried to maintain my composure as a caring physician.

"Then, one day at the hospital in Prishlatar, something happened that changed my attitude irreversibly. I was called to the Emergency Room to find Vladic there. A member of the NATO peacekeeping force had beaten him nearly to death for trading in contraband goods, including weapons.

"He died the following day of head injuries.

"I became bent on revenge.

"I drove the next day into the countryside to the headquarters of the KLA and offered my services in exchange for their help in finding my brother's killer. When I described the circumstances, the commander told me: "There can only be one person on the NATO force responsible for this. His name is Korporaal Pieter Van De Poel, a Belgian. He is a known sadist, especially towards women. He rivals the Serbs, themselves."

She went on: "I spent a week with the KLA training unit, where I shared my medical knowledge and they taught me to shoot, to kill with a knife and also how to construct Improvised Explosive Devices using cell phones as triggers."

That reminded me of something. I looked into a cleft in the basement wall and saw what I was looking for: a small cordless drill and a soldering gun, a loop of unused solder draped over the drill.

Marijke's color was fading as she slipped into shock - or was something else at play here?

She continued, in evident pain, and why she went on with this confession, I didn't know - but I continued to record: "The KLA eventually recruited me into their organ harvest program. We would strip our Serb prisoners of their kidneys at the by now notorious 'Red House' facility at the Albanian border. It housed a full surgical facility and a system for transporting organs along with villagers who would receive them from a local airport in the mountain highlands, to Istanbul, where transplantation would take place.

"There was no money for anti-rejection drugs for patients post-transplant, so an elaborate and clandestine tissue typing program was set up by KLA loyalists at the University Hospital in Prishlatar. Excellent matches were made between the prisoners and members of my village, amongst others."

In some significant pain, she went into depth about how the ABO blood groups, Human Lymphocyte Antigen (HLA System) and Kelly and Duffy antigen groups were carefully matched. This was getting out of hand.

She then said: "We removed hundreds of organs from these prisoners. Sometimes, we would remove the kidneys on one day, then bring them back, days later, before uremia had completely set in, and we would eviscerate them, taking heart, lungs, pancreas and intestines to repay our Istanbul transplant colleagues for taking care of the kidney transplants needed in Ksro. The prisoners would enter the Red House crying, asking us to please not carve them up before they died. We listened to none of this. We just did our work and if we only took their kidneys, we put a bullet in their heads.

"This went on for months, until there were no more prisoners. Near the end of this period, I dyed my hair blonde to disguise myself.

"That evening I followed Pieter and his colleagues to what I had learned was their favorite bar in Prishlatar. It was run by a Belgian expatriate and was very popular with the NATO troops as a place to drink, dance and pick up local girls. I went alone that night, wearing a revealing dress and carrying an important little red purse on a long shoulder chain. I sat close to Pieter, who eventually began buying me drinks (which I would switch for the ever-empty glass of the woman sitting next to me. She became very drunk in the course of that night, as you can imagine).

"I waited until Pieter had finished drinking shots of Ouzo with his friends before I truly entered into conversation with him. I introduced myself as a local housekeeper. He shared with me his rural background in Flanders, told me about Lark Farm and indicated that if I ever wanted to work in Belgium, his mother Paula was always looking for 'help' from Eastern bloc women. They worked for so much less than Belgians.

"I told him that I would think about it, but first, would he like to dance?

"He looked about, realized his friends were gone and that the dance floor was nearly empty. He winked at the bartender and took me by the hand. We danced a few fast numbers and then, during a long slow dance, I removed a syrette from my purse and, while spanking him on the buttock in a very forward gesture, injected him with 100 mg of Somnescine, a rapid-onset, long-acting drug that creates dissociation of thought from action. When under the influence of Somnescine, a person becomes docile and suggestible but fully capable of physical activity. It also creates amnesia.

"Pieter did not discern the injection from the spanking and in fact suggested (certainly as a consequence of the latter) that he and I leave the bar together to 'spend a little additional time getting to know one another.' He asked me to leave first so that no one would see us leaving together: a reputation issue, I assumed. I watched through the window as he paid the bartender. When he reached the sidewalk, the drug's effect had already begun.

"'Pieter,' I asked, 'how would you like to come to my place for the evening?' He indicated that he would enjoy that. We got in my car and I began to drive. Soon thereafter, he closed his eyes and slept as I drove us all the way to the Red House, one hundred kilometers distant. My colleagues helped me bind his hands and feet before we brought him into a holding cell in the building, where we drew his blood and had it rushed back to the lab in Prishlatar for typing.

"When he woke up, hung over and tied like a hog, I explained who I was, that I knew he had murdered my brother and that I was now going to coolly murder him, by removing his living organs, one by one. Wide-eyed, he began screaming and never really stopped until we anesthetized him later that day. Word had come in from Prishlatar that he was quite a prize - his was the rarest of antigen profiles - *AB+*, *Kelly+*, *Duffy+* - exactly the match that four of my nieces in Ksro had been waiting for and certainly that of several Turkish patients who would benefit from heart, lung and digestive organ transplants at his expense.

"I took his kidneys out through sub costal incisions on his back and had them transported immediately along with two of my nieces to Istanbul (the four nieces had to draw lots amongst themselves to see who would get the organs). I packed his wounds with acidic dressings, just to enhance his pain. I watched and waited for two days, just to see him suffer maximally. I then returned him to the Operating Room and took his eyes out for their corneas, one by one, using only a paralytic agent and no anesthesia. Then, a day later, we took all the rest of his organs of interest and shipped them to Istanbul. I then personally took his body to a former weapons cave on the Kosovo-Albanian border that just crawled with rats. I dragged him in and watched for hours as they devoured him."

She then continued: "So I suppose you wonder how and why I found my way to Lark Farm?"

I nodded.

"There was a good chance that one or both of his parents would have tissues of the same type as Pieter. Also, my sense of revenge remained unquenched. I was literally bloodthirsty. So, for a time, I dyed my hair back to its normal color and returned to my hospital duties. Months after Pieter's absence was known and accepted, I wrote a note to Paula, at Lark Farm. I indicated that I had been a housekeeper at the NATO Barracks in Prishlatar and that Pieter and I had known one another before he left unexpectedly. I included in my note that he had suggested a long time ago that I should ask Paula if she ever needed help at Lark Farm when the NATO force left Kosovo, which they recently had. I explained that I had grown up poor in a Kosovar village and had never traveled, so it would be exciting for me to see Belgium and perhaps more, should she ever have a position available.

"I included in the letter his *NATO Service Award* which, I explained, I was going to sew onto his uniform on the day that he went missing. I told her that I was sorry for her loss and that I was sure that she would want this memento of his service.

"Paula immediately responded to my letter," she went on. "She paid my expenses to come to Lark Farm on a trial basis to see if I would enjoy working as her maid in the B&B. That was several years ago. So I came and became a fixture in the B&B. Over the years, my colleagues gradually supplied me with the surgical instruments and medications I would need to accomplish my task.

"I watched and waited for an opportunity to obtain blood from both Paula and Thijs for tissue typing. Paula's turn came late one night only recently when she was alone and had been drinking (she had been struggling with her decision to leave Thijs). After a little injection of Somnescine when I bumped into her, apologizing profusely, I drew her blood. The result? *A+, Kelly-, Duffy-*. No good. She immediately became expendable, in my mind. That she was having an affair with de Smet under Thijs's nose did nothing to enhance my sympathy for her. After all, she had given birth to my brother's murderer. I have simple but strong emotions. I learned to hate her.

With Thijs, the sample of blood came in the oddest way. Last week, he came running into the house with a massive nosebleed. He had been plowing a section of the field when his blood pressure must have jumped suddenly and he burst an artery in his nasal septum. I packed his nose briefly with an Iodoform gauze laced with Somnescine, which traverses mucous membranes readily. This did not stop the bleeding but it did allow me to collect some nasal drippings without his awareness into a heparinized blood collection tube from a kit I was able to retrieve and fill before I packed his nose tightly. I had him rest until the bleeding was then well resolved.

My mind was racing. This was the easiest confession I had ever elicited. Why?

"That afternoon, the tube was on ice and in the post to my colleagues in Prishlatar. Two days later, the answer came: *AB+, Kelly+, Duffy+*. It was then just a matter of opportunity. You know what happened next.

"Three unique events converged. Thijs uncovered the Big Bertha shell, Helen MacCormick was careless with her cell phone and Thijs was planning on plowing the rear field on the fateful day. It was always his habit, when plowing back there, to have me let him know when the Bomb Disposal Battalion was coming by. I think he liked de Smet and was tolerant of his relationship with Paula but wanted to limit their time alone, when possible."

Thijs groaned on the table then resumed a gentle snore, small droplets of blood issuing from his back incision.

"Late that night, I was inspecting the Big Bertha shell in the darkness when you returned from *De Salient*. I waited until your room lights were out for an hour before I came in here and drilled access holes, soldered the wires to the cell phone battery and attached it to a makeshift detonator that I created from a smaller shell and placed it next to the critical position on the larger shell to assure its co-detonation. I think I may have made a little noise at the door when I returned to the B&B because I heard you stirring in your room. I froze in the hallway for an hour before returning to my bed.

It was my sense of irony that made me program the phone system so that it was actually Thijs who killed his wife when he called the Lark Farm number. I also thought this might implicate him perfectly. Apparently not," she said as she looked up at me with venom.

For a moment, I ignored her obvious temporizing maneuver as I thought my way through it.

"I knew that you did it when I heard the initial report, " I said.

"How could you have known?"

"No one in Flanders wears a full length woolen coat on a hot day except someone who expects to be struck by flying glass."

She looked up, astonished.

I went on "So I assume that you had syrettes of Somnescine in that woolen coat at the time of the blast and you injected Thijs with one of them once you were settled into your hospital rooms."

She nodded.

"And you had prepositioned a black Yugo in the parking garage of Jan Yperman hospital, didn't you?"

She nodded again.

"And you planned to take his kidneys in that ice bucket to Prishlatar yourself, didn't you."

Again, she nodded.

"So," I asked her, finally deducing the reason for her volubility: "Where is the detonator?"

"What detonator?" she asked as she grimaced in pain and anger.

"I know that you have prolonged this confession so that your pre-planned cover explosion will include me, so where is it and when is it programmed to go off? I am sure that you could have had those kidneys out in twenty minutes and I am also sure that you would have used the impending explosion to hasten your pace, so we must be close to the time that you set. Where is it?"

Then she smiled. "Find it yourself."

With that, I saw her insert one of the barbs of the wire that encircled her chest and arms into the soft skin in front of her left elbow. Immediately adjacent to the tendon on the front side of the elbow, it is the site in the human body that is least likely to be the focus of blunt trauma. She looked up at me with eyes of hate and said one last thing before twisting her arms painfully, driving a metal thorn into that protected cavity and against a fragile glass canister, buried there.

"My family will eventually find you. And they will take their revenge upon you, Mr. Nigel Hendrick. It is our custom."

In the next seconds, the room was filled with the almond scent of cyanide, released from the chamber embedded in her arm and dispelled by her lungs after its rapid absorption and circulation. Marijke turned first blue and then a red shade - and was gone. The KLA had done more than train her. They had equipped her for suicide.

I knew that her prolonged confession had been intended to make me tarry long enough to be exposed to an explosion that would remove all evidence of Thijs and this latest organ harvest, as I had seen the wires near the shell outside when I tipped it to its side. Her timing was excellent. I tore the drapes from Thijs' back, and there it was, Marijke's cell phone in his back pocket, the display noting a countdown at fifteen seconds and declining.

There was no time to both carry Thijs and exit this trap in sufficient time to avoid the explosion. And I was not going to leave him behind.

"Sorry Thijs," I said, as I lifted the sword high, cutting face forward, and brought it down fully upon the cell phone, cleaving it and the center of Thijs' right buttock in half. Like a snake without its head, the timer in the cell phone was disconnected from the battery, which also separated from its lightly soldered wires.

Thankfully, Marijke had not wired a contingent explosive system.

Thijs was apparently more observant of attacks upon his buttock than upon his back, as he immediately awoke and tried to sit up - a good thing, as that maneuver put pressure on his new wound's bleeders. I knew that Thijs, in a few days, would be stunned to learn that at least parts of Pieter remained alive in distant Kosovo and Turkey but I was reluctant to speak to him about it now.

At that moment, the guard groggily entered the basement and tried to take in the grisly scene. I turned off the recorder on his service device, handed it to him, asked him to save it as evidence and to call an ambulance and the coroner. He began executing these duties as I, unsteadily, marched past him, around the farm building, found Max, turned on his light and pedaled slowly back up the gentle Passchendaele Ridge to *De Salient*.

Chapter 21. Nostos

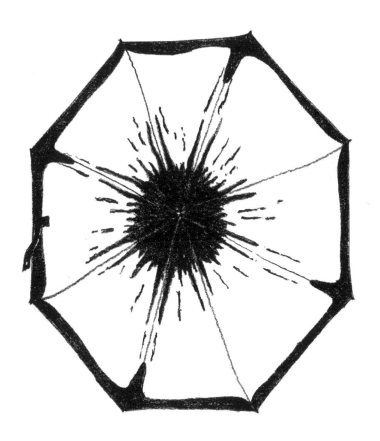

When I attended high school in Kent, the Jesuits taught me Classical Greek for three years.

They thought that the Greek language was perhaps the most important bit of wisdom they could impart to a young man. My version of scholarship lay in the retention of the stories we translated, not in the language itself. One of the great foci of the Greek epics was the concept of "Nostos," or "Return." It was perhaps best personified in the tale of Odysseus, who spent ten years in a tortuous return from the Trojan War, enduring the Furies, the Cyclops Polyphemus and Scylla and Carybdis along the way. Once he arrived at his home on Ithaca, he confronted the suitors in his home while disguised and he stunned them all when he was able to fulfill his wife Penelope's challenge of shooting an arrow through the apertures of ten aligned axe heads.

As I climbed aboard Max that morning at *De Salient*, I only hoped that my voyage homeward would not be so tumultuous. Or at least that is how I expressed myself in an email to Emil over my breakfast. In it, I went on at length about all that I had experienced in Flanders, how it contrasted with how little I had expected when I had arrived and how much these past few days had awakened me.

Although I felt a yearning to be home, I also felt an attraction to these low lying lands and all the history that they experienced, little by little, over this past century and the history that they would continue to engender in the centuries to come.

Last night, after the Emergency Services team from Jan Yperman Hospital had once again taken Marijke and Thijs away, she to be prepared for autopsy and burial, he to be put back together in the Operating Room, I returned to *De Salient*. There, the Canadian General was happily pouring drinks for the Belgian Bomb Disposal Battalion, who had come to continue to celebrate the memory of their colleague, De Smet. Of course, Wouter and team were in the back room, feasting on braised chicken legs in brandied gravy and drinking scads of Passendale Ale. They loved solved cases. I mentioned Marijke's dying threats to Wouter, all of which he discounted.

He was, after all, happily in his cups.

Wouter and I sat together well into the night, he thanking me profusely for my efforts on the case and admonishing me for my carelessness with my life. When I turned to Wouter and thought all of the recent events through, a tear came to my eye, which, as he watched, I was able to absorb into that former arid self of mine. Then, a second came. And a third.

Wouter called the Canadian General over to the table and demanded a whisky for his stricken friend. Then, with a sip, the tears stopped, and I smiled. I thought of the Ell room and the little nook with the wine, and I hoped that Thijs would put the B&B right again, even without Paula's distinct personality. I recalled sitting there days ago, before initially reuniting with Wouter, thinking that my few days in Flanders would consist of cycle touring to dead old historic sites, eating French food in German quantities and drinking too much Belgian beer. The contrast between then and now had grown as a consequence of unanticipated circumstances, of course, but also as a result of a queer opening of myself to things that I had previously not beheld. I committed myself to hanging on to this point of view, even as I hugged Wouter to say goodbye and shambled off to bed.

There, on the pillow, lay a small Christmas ornament, though Christmas was months away. It was a little metal bicycle, painted with red nail polish, sitting astride a note that said:

"With Great Admiration For A Modern Warrior."

- **The Staff of the Moorslede Center for Molecular Forensics**

I slipped the ornament into my shirt pocket, to be able to have it near me on my ride home in the morning. After sleeping peacefully, I awoke early, had breakfast, stepped outside into bright Flanders sunshine and secured my saddlebags to Max.

Soon, he and I were on Grenadiersstraat, making the left turn onto Vierde Regiment Karabienersstraat and its gentle decline to the New British Commonwealth Cemetery. I made one more stop there, said goodbye to McCrae and the other poets and looked long and hard for the ghosts of Liggett Storer and DEQQUND KNoRS, but they were now apparently at peace. I signed the logbook one last time with the words "Thank God I Came." I thought of Emil as I did so.

The wind was blowing in from the northeast, and I knew what that meant. Time to put some distance between me and this haunted land.

Max and I set forth once again onto 's Graventafelstraat before making the left turn onto Passendalesteenweg for the brief ride to Westrozebeke and from there onto Sint Elooistraat, which, after some additional meandering on side streets, took us to the Houthulst Forest. We stood by the edge of the forest and peered within. In the light fog, Max and I witnessed the scurrying about of German soldiers, preparing to fire a Big Bertha howitzer toward Ypres. Then, with a slight swirl of the wind, the fog cleared and we saw the familiar uniforms of the Belgian Bomb Disposal Battalion as they readied the day's collections and discharges. Several recognized Max and waved. I waved back and as I did so, Max's front light flickered on for a second.

"I really do have to fix that short in his light," I noted to myself, as I pushed off.

By lunchtime, Max and I had reached the coast at Middelkerke, then turned northeast, dined in Oostende at a cafe that faced in the general direction of Calgary and reached Zeebrugge for the evening ferry with plenty of time to spare. As I passed the roadside shrines en route to the ferry, I expressed thanks not only for my health but also for the grand experiences of my life, this trip to Flanders being just the latest.

I tucked Max into a secure spot on the ferry's car deck and returned to the bar for the long night ride. As I was heading back to the UK, I immediately ordered a Lagavulin scotch, just to reacquaint myself with the Auld Sod.

OK, I eventually did have four glasses.

As I set into my second glass, I pulled the dog-eared *Untold Tales of the Ypres Salient* from my saddlebag. Although I had read it periodically throughout my trip, I knew I would never finish it. My first-hand exposure to Flanders was simply too compelling. I did look into the Appendix to see if it mentioned Liggett, his brothers, DEQQUND or even Lark Farm. I was surprised to find only a brief reference to Lark Farm. It seems that its German occupiers reported hearing odd noises at night there and feared that spirits occupied the place. No justification for the entry was given. Just the odd mention.

Once again, I fell asleep on the bench beside the bar for an hour or two before later gratefully finding my way to and entrenching myself in my berth, fully clothed. As the seas pounded out their fury on our ship, I slept like a dead man. When I awoke, we were in the harbor in Hull. It was the most peaceful, beautiful English morning I could remember having seen in quite a while. I enjoyed a scone and Earl Grey tea in the market near the railway station, and then Max and I climbed aboard the express train to London.

It was early evening when we arrived at King's Cross Station. Max and I adjusted ourselves to riding in city traffic, first along Euston Rd., then Marylebone Rd., followed by a left turn onto Sussex Gardens and then on to the grounds of Hyde Park. Soon after we entered the Park, we made a stop at The Long Water and watched the birds for a bit. They were all there: Little Grebes, Ospreys, Skylarks and Tufted Ducks.

I was at home. Or nearly so.

Max and I found our way through the park to Exhibition Rd. which we followed to Cromwell Rd., took a left there, continued past the Victoria and Albert Museum onto Thurloe Place and finally Brompton Rd. With Harrods's lights just coming on in the near distance, we turned right onto Beauchamp Place, past my favorite Portuguese and Lebanese restaurants and on to its end, where it branched into three streets. We turned left onto the very short stem known as Devonshire Rd. and pulled up to number 125, lying small but stately in the darkening evening.

The last pedal strokes of a long journey are bittersweet.

Of course, with the exertion done, there is pleasure. However, it becomes clear that there is pleasure in the pain of the journey, too. Or at least, these were my thoughts as I walked Max up the driveway to the garage. With some reluctance, I slid the key into the garage door, opened it and entered. Just before the trip, I had constructed a rack for Max, so I removed my saddlebags and lifted him onto its yoke. I noticed that when he was installed there, his handlebars lay just next to a window facing the kitchen window, eight feet distant.

"Good," I thought. "This way I can keep an eye on the old fellow when I dine."

Then, when I released my grip on his handlebars, Max made the usual desultory front wheel turn to a resting position, facing the window. As he did so, his headlight flashed and for a brief second lit up the kitchen window.

Now, I know that I had seen plenty of ghosts on this trip, but the Investigator in me could have sworn that I saw someone duck down in the kitchen, out of the light. With some care, I picked up a tire iron, exited and closed the garage door and went to the side door of the house.

The door was very slightly ajar.

When I opened the door, I smelled something that immediately took me back to *De Salient*. At first, I could not place it - it was a pleasant, deep, rich smell - as though something delicious was being cooked. I stepped carefully within and chose not to turn on any lights as I slowly stepped down the hall, since the evening was still just light enough to allow me to find my way. I crept slowly toward the kitchen, wondering what mad Kosovar I might meet in my own castle.

Yet, I kept on, just as I had at Lark Farm. Was I mad?

When I turned the corner to the kitchen, I was both blinded by a powerful light and stunned by a loud popping sound that I assumed had to be the discharge of a gun. It took just a moment for my eyes to adjust to a fabulous display of crimson before me, which I took to be from an aortic explosion - or worse.

Then, realizing that I remained whole, I looked up into the face of a gigantic red poppy.

It was the umbrella that I had mailed from the *In Flanders Fields* museum, fully opened.

And its tip was pointing toward me.

As I looked to the left and quickly equated the scent with what was on the stove, I realized that it was Flemish stew.

My favorite.

Then, as I stood breathless, tire iron in hand, the umbrella was slowly lowered and behind it I saw a woman. She had blonde (well, slightly gray) hair, tied in a bun, slightly protruding ears, a lithe body clad in a form-fitting white apron and a beautiful bow of a mouth.

It was Lois.

She looked at me intently and was, for a moment, silent.

She then turned to the right, exposing two bottles of beer on the table behind her - one, a Passendale Ale, the other, a Boezinge.

"I don't know about you," she said, "But I am having the Boezinge."

I was astonished and about to speak when she stopped me, placed an arm on mine, leaned into me (at which time I perceived the subtle scent of perfume) and said, "Nigel, Emil Lazarus violated your trust. He has been keeping me well informed of your experiences in Flanders. Hearing them awakened me from my folly and from my selfishness. Especially your poem about the war. I realized how wrong I had been in my perception of you. And how very much I need you."

I set the tire iron down and said nothing as I took all of this in. It was too quick and it was too unbelievable but I had also been through the same in the past days and this rate of change had now become normal. I listened.

Then, Lois said: "Please, please...will you have me back, Nigel?"

Before I could answer, a flashing light in the near distance startled me. It was Max's headlight flashing. Again. And again.

I took Lois in my arms and as I smiled, I also wept. In my last moments of objective thinking before I released myself to this experience, I thought, "There is no greater return than that which has been deemed forever lost."

Then, first a Boezinge and afterwards, a Passendale, lost their caps. From each came a brief plume of carbonated mist that first rose, then swirled, then broke into a million pieces before becoming lost, forever.

The End

About The Author

Peter C. Johnson, MD, a reconstructive surgeon and medical technology executive, lives in Raleigh, NC.